Gold, Maya.

Harriet the spy, double agent

	DATE DUE		

HARRIET
THE SPY®,
DOUBLE AGENT

Other books featuring Harriet the Spy® and her friends

Harriet the Spy

Harriet Spies Again

The Long Secret

Sport

Written by

Maya Gold

Based on the characters created by Louise Fitzhugh

DELACORTE PRESS

Published by
Delacorte Press
an imprint of
Random House Children's Books
a division of Random House, Inc.
New York

Visit us on the Web! www.randomhouse.com/kids
Educators and librarians, for a variety of teaching tools, visit us at
www.randomhouse.com/teachers

Library of Congress Cataloging-in-Publication Data
Gold, Maya.
Harriet the spy, double agent / Maya Gold.
p. cm.
Summary: While spying on her New York City neighborhood with a new friend, Annie, twelve-year-old Harriet decides that the only way to learn Annie's many secrets is to spy on her, as well.
ISBN 0-385-32787-0 (trade) — ISBN 0-385-90294-8 (glb)
[1. Spies—Fiction. 2. Secrets—Fiction. 3. Friendship—Fiction. 4. Schools—Fiction. 5. Christmas—Fiction. 6. New York (N.Y.)—Fiction.] I. Title.
PZ7.G5628Har 2005
[Fic]—dc22
2004021336

The text of this book is set in 12.5-point Goudy.
Book design by Trish P. Watts
Printed in the United States of America
September 2005
10 9 8 7 6 5 4 3 2 1
BVG

ACKNOWLEDGMENTS

Grateful thanks to my agent, Phyllis Wender, and the wonderful staff at Rosenstone/Wender agency; to my editor, Beverly Horowitz, for her astute and gracious guidance; to Louise Fitzhugh for creating such marvelous characters; to Lois Morehead for her enthusiastic thumbs-up; to Susie and Ellen Cohen for reading every word with patient care; to Laura Shaine Cunningham and her writer daughters, Alexandra and Jasmine, for their ardent support; and to my parents and brothers for making my childhood such a joy. Finally, bottomless thanks to my daughter and first reader, Sophia, for her excellent writing advice and soul-warming smile, and to her circle of friends at Marbletown Elementary School and Rondout Valley Middle School for reminding me daily how children speak, think, and feel.

CHAPTER 1

Harriet M. Welsch took out the flashlight that always hung from her spy belt, snapped off the overhead light, and stepped into the bathtub. It was precisely 9:29 p.m. It felt strange to stand in the tub fully dressed (except for her sneakers, which would not do), but spies were accustomed to doing strange things. Harriet peered through the narrow exhaust window, set over a twin row of black and white checkered tiles, and hoped that her contact, the girl with four names, understood the importance of promptness.

A faint glow of peach-tinted streetlight shone through the pane. Harriet stared over the treetops of East Eighty-seventh Street at the carved marble cornices on the south side of the street. It was snowing again, and a light stripe of powder lined every bare twig. She wished they'd agreed on an earlier time. Nine-thirty was dangerously close to her bedtime, when one of her parents might venture up to the third floor to bid her a distracted goodnight. Revise, she informed herself. First thing tomorrow. She narrowed her eyes, squinting into the snowfall.

A circle of light snapped on in a dark window across the street. Could that be it? The angle looked lower than Harriet had expected. She held her breath as the new light snapped off and on twice more. The signal!

Harriet lifted her flashlight and clicked her switch in the same pattern. A grin spread across her face. It *works*, she thought, already starting to dream up a message code far more complex than a simple flash-three for "I'm here." Didn't sailors have some kind of code alphabet, like those colorful flags that flapped over Long Island yacht clubs and showed up on beach towels? Semaphore, that was the name for it. She and the girl with four names could invent an East Eighty-seventh Street semaphore, with different flashlight patterns for every letter.

The phone rang in the hall. Harriet jumped from the tub, singing out, "It's for me!" before her mother could pick up downstairs. She skidded into the hallway and grabbed the receiver, tucking it into her shoulder as she pulled the long cord through her bedroom door. "It worked!"

"What worked?" The voice was a boy's.

"Sport?"

"Of course. What worked?"

"Nothing," said Harriet, hoping she sounded blasé. "I thought you were Annie."

"Oh," said Sport. "Annie." The crack in his voice, one note childlike and one newly husky, made him sound like a bad country singer. "How can her real name be Annie Smith? Annie *Smith.*"

"So?" Harriet twisted the phone cord around her left thumb. She didn't approve of repeating oneself, aloud or in prose. Harriet was going to be a writer, and she knew that every word mattered. Her best friend, Sport, who dreamed about playing first base for the Mets, was not as precise. She had high hopes for Annie, however. The signal had flashed at exactly nine-thirty.

Annie had moved to their neighborhood back in September, under mysterious circumstances. The two-doctor couple across the street, Morris and Barbara Feigenbaum, who had houseplants and patients instead of children, had taken in Barbara's twelve-year-old niece. This new neighbor had introduced herself to Harriet as Rosarita Sauvage, to her moony-eyed schoolmate Sport as Yolanda Montezuma, and to others as Zoe Carpaccio. It had come as a shock to discover, a few days before at Thanksgiving dinner, that all three of these remarkable names belonged to the same girl, whose birth name was duller than toast.

But Annie herself had potential. The girl had created not one but three new identities, each with a personality to match. There was also the unanswered question of why she'd been expelled from Sport's school, and transferred to Harriet's, just a few weeks before Christmas vacation. She must have done something *outrageous*, thought Harriet, and I'm going to find out what it was. That might have been a tall order for some seventh graders, but Harriet M. Welsch was an experienced spy. Ever since she could print, she had taken extensive notes in a series of green composition books, which she kept locked in a trunk at the foot of her bed. "A writer needs to know everything," her former nanny, Ole Golly, had said many times. "It's all grist for the mill."

"I'm not sure I can love a plain Annie," Sport sighed. "She's such a Yolanda."

"Get used to it," Harriet snapped, trying to hide her impatience. Falling out of love over a name seemed as flimsy as Sport's claim that he'd fallen in love with Yolanda's green shoes. Harriet wondered if Sport knew what love really meant.

Not that she was an expert on love. Ole Golly had sidestepped Harriet's questions in every phase of her courtship, estrangement, and joyous reunion with her husband, George Waldenstein, and Harriet's parents restricted themselves to tossing off the occasional "Love you," as if prefacing it with an "I" would take too much of an effort. Maybe I ought to try spying on someone in love, Harriet thought, if it doesn't involve too much kissing. She disliked long kisses in movies, which always made her wonder what the two actors had eaten for dinner.

"Listen," she said, "I'm on an assignment from Grenville. I'm walking plain Annie to school in the morning. If you'd like to meet us, arrive at the corner of East End by eight-twenty-three. Let's synchronize our watches."

"What?"

Harriet sighed. Sport had known her since preschool, and it drove her crazy when he didn't recognize everyday spy terminology. She felt this was part of his job as best friend. "Make sure we both have the same time. What does your watch say?"

"Nine-thirty-two," said Sport.

"Two minutes slow. Fix it," said Harriet, and hung up. She liked to hang up without saying goodbye. It made her last words sound important. She went to the trunk and took out a green notebook, her twenty-first.

SPORT IS NO LONGER CONVINCED OF HIS FEELINGS FOR ANNIE. IF HE STILL WENT TO MY SCHOOL AND HAD MR. GRENVILLE FOR ENGLISH, I'D REMIND HIM OF THE LINE IN ROMEO AND JULIET, ACT 2: "THAT WHICH WE CALL A ROSE BY ANY OTHER NAME WOULD SMELL AS SWEET." SURELY THE SAME MUST BE TRUE FOR A GIRL WITH GREEN SHOES.

• • •

Annie Smith wasn't wearing the green shoes when Harriet crossed the street to escort her from Dr. and Dr. Feigenbaum's snowy front stoop to the Gregory School. Annie had put on black boots and a charcoal wool coat that Rosarita Sauvage would have shunned as too sensible. The only promising touches were a scarlet beret, worn a bit to one side, and a long chenille scarf.

"Where'd you get those weird mittens, H'spy?" was her greeting.

"They're not mittens, they're fingerless gloves," answered Harriet, wiggling the tips of her fingers. "They give me the freedom to write without freezing my hands."

"You look like Fagin," said Annie, "from *Oliver Twist*."

She's read Charles Dickens, thought Harriet, or at least seen the movie *Oliver!* That's another good sign. She remembered that Mr. Grenville had asked her to "take Annie under her wing" because they were both avid readers. We may have more in common than that, she thought, noting that Annie plowed straight through the puddles the same way she did, as if product-testing her waterproof boots.

There was always a lake of gray slush at the corner of East Eighty-seventh Street. Some of the cars were still covered with soot-crusted snow. They must have been parked in those spots since the Thanksgiving blizzard. There were piles of heavyweight plastic bags next to most of the garbage cans set on the curb; the storm had delayed morning pickup. "I wonder how many turkey carcasses you could exhume on the East Side this morning?" said Annie.

"Scads," replied Harriet, pleased with the verb *exhume*. "Next month there'll be Christmas trees everywhere, fluttering tinsel." A very large man with a very small dog in a red and white sweater bent down to lift the creature over the slush puddle.

"Look at that guy," she whispered, angling her head toward the man and his candy-striped poodle.

"It's Simon LaRocque," Annie said, "from my ex-school."

"Just Rocque. No La." Harriet turned from the

dog man to wave at Sport, whose hair, she noticed, was carefully parted and combed. Maybe he'd made his peace with Yolanda's real name. "Hi, Sport."

Sport nodded, tongue-tied. He seemed to be staring at Annie's beret. Annie ignored him, turning to Harriet.

"Hey, H'spy, why do you call Simon Sport?"

"Same reason you call me H'spy."

"That's your *name*."

"Well, Sport is *his* name."

"I used to like football," Sport mumbled. "When I was a kid."

"I'm glad you outgrew it," said Annie. "Football's for morons." She stepped into the deepest part of the corner puddle, sending twin waves of slush into the crosswalk. Harriet followed suit. Sport, who was wearing his usual black Converse hightops, looked embarrassed at having to step to one side. The three of them strode across East End Avenue. Buses and taxis were lined up at every red light.

"So tell me about this Gregory School," Annie said as she sloshed through the half-frozen lake on the opposite corner. "Who do I need to look out for?"

"Our homeroom is mostly decent. It's all girls this year, so you missed Pinky Whitehead and the Boy with the Purple Socks. But there's still the Marion

Hawthorne Experience." Harriet shuddered. "A legend in her own mind. And her faithful sidekicks, Rachel the Bland and Carrie the Clone. They won't pick on you unless Marion does."

"Sounds like a pack of snobs." Annie kicked the wrought-iron railing that skirted a sycamore tree.

"You'll be fine," said Harriet. "Just don't act peculiar."

"I'm never peculiar," Annie said with a sniff. "You must mean Rosarita or Zoe."

"I thought you were Zoe when you felt estranged."

"When did I say that?"

"Thanksgiving," said Sport. Annie glanced over her shoulder, as if she'd forgotten he was walking behind them. Sport blushed the color of Annie's beret.

"I'm not estranged, Simon," she said. "I'm actually feeling quite rakish." She flung her scarf over one shoulder and swept ahead. Sport started after her with a lovestruck expression, but Harriet laid a firm hand on his arm.

"Your school is that way," she said, pointing south down the avenue. Sport looked embarrassed again. He nodded, hefting his backpack, and trudged down the sidewalk without a word. This nonsense has *got* to stop, Harriet thought, with her hands on her hips.

She was vastly relieved when Sport lifted a small chunk of ice with the toe of one sneaker and started to dribble it soccer style, bobbing and weaving through the pedestrians.

She caught up to Annie in just a few strides. "Did you see my signal last night?" she asked.

"It was excellent," Annie said. "Silly, but excellent."

Harriet drew herself up at that "silly." So much for making up semaphore signals together, she thought, feeling miffed. She was still searching for just the right dignified comeback when they reached the Gregory School. The wide steps in front had been swept clear of snow, leaving big shapeless drifts on both sides and gray sprinkles of rock salt atop the wet granite. Students clustered in twos and threes, notebooks clutched to their chests, comparing Thanksgiving vacations. Several heads swiveled to see who was arriving with Harriet Welsch. Annie glanced around anxiously, lifting a hand to adjust her coat collar. "The bloody Bastille," she muttered.

Marion Hawthorne turned toward them, swathed in a very expensive-looking white coat and silk scarf that her mother must have bought in Europe.

"Marion," said Harriet, making her voice sound commanding. "This is my friend, and our new homeroom classmate—"

"Cassandra," said Annie Smith, tossing her hair back from under her scarlet beret. "I'm Cassandra D'Amore."

• • •

"Why did you say that?" hissed Harriet. They were hanging up coats and stashing wet boots in the lockers just outside homeroom.

Annie shrugged, slipping her feet into loafers. "Free country, the last I heard."

"Yes, but—"

"So mind your own business." Annie walked through the door and stood there uncertainly, wondering which desk would be hers. See if I help you, thought Harriet, stung for the second time. She sat down at her desk, between Janie Gibbs and Beth Ellen Hansen. Mr. Grenville was already crossing the room to the new student, with a wide smile in place.

"There you are, so good to see you," he burbled. "I'm Mr. Grenville, homeroom and English, and this'll be your desk." He pulled back a chair, catty-corner from Harriet's. Annie sat down without looking her way.

Mr. Grenville went back to the head of the classroom and turned to address the group. "Everybody, I'd like you all to meet Annie Smith."

Marion Hawthorne swiveled to face her. "Annie?" she said. "You told me your name was—"

"Cassandra D'Amore. It is."

Mr. Grenville frowned. "My attendance chart lists you as Annie Smith. Would that be . . . a nickname?"

Marion smirked and Beth Ellen Hansen leaned forward. Let's see how she handles *this* one, thought Harriet.

"You might call it a nickname," said Annie coolly. "In certain, er, federal circles."

Marion's eyes widened. Beth Ellen looked frightened.

Mr. Grenville's thick eyebrows rose high on his forehead. His voice sounded richly amused. "Or we might call it something else—for example, a genre of writing including novels, short stories, novellas, and experimental forms. Which is?" He looked straight at Harriet.

"Fiction," she answered.

Mr. Grenville smiled. He had kind eyes. "Would that be correct, Annie?"

She didn't blink. "Names have been changed to protect the innocent. That's all I'm permitted to say on the matter."

Mr. Grenville made a small bow from the waist, and Harriet thought, as she often had, that he must have once yearned for a life on the stage. "All right, then, Cassandra D'Amore. We're reading *Romeo and Juliet*. Are you familiar?"

"Montagues hate the Capulets, Capulets hate the Montagues, everyone dies." Annie nodded.

There's more to her than meets the eye, Harriet thought. She's very well-read for an impolite person who lies a lot. Annie Smith was a woman of multiple mysteries: not just the reason for her expulsion from Sport's public school, but the reason she'd come to live with her uncle and aunt in the first place. Where were her *parents*?

Harriet narrowed her eyes to slits and stared at the back of Annie Smith's head, noting the way her pink-rimmed ears stuck through her hair. I'm going to find out all your secrets, she vowed, and the thought of it made her deliciously happy. I'm going to start spying on *you*.

• • •

WHY ARE THE FEIGENBAUMS SHELTERING ANNIE? IS SHE RUDE TO THEM? SHE APPEARS TO BE FOND OF THEIR CAT.

Harriet paused for a moment, the tip of her pen in her mouth. She could practically hear Ole Golly exhorting her, "Write with your brain, not your tongue." She set the pen back on the page and thought for a moment before she continued.

NICE TO CATS ISN'T ENOUGH, she wrote, closing the notebook. She set it back in her trunk and turned the small key in its brass clasp. Her room was, as always, in order, her clothes for the following day folded neatly on top of her dresser. Spies needed to keep their possessions in readiness. One never knew when one might need to follow a lead on short notice.

She changed into her new flannel pajamas, the ones that were cut like her father's, with notched lapels. She imagined herself strolling onto the set of a black-and-white Hollywood movie, something with Katharine Hepburn and dark marble floors. Who is that dashing young woman? Not *dashing*, she decided, editing herself as she headed into the bathroom to brush her teeth. *Insouciant*. Yes, that was the word.

She squeezed the paste onto her toothbrush and looked at herself in the mirror. Not insouciant, either, she thought. The word for this outfit is *baggy*.

Harriet brushed, rinsed, and spit, set her toothbrush back into the rack and her glass in its usual spot, and switched off the light. A movement outside caught her eye. She stepped into the bathtub and peered out the window in time for the second and third flashes. Semaphore.

Harriet woke feeling happy, remembering the inspiration that had come to her just before sleep. She'd been lying in bed for what seemed like a very long time, trying to make herself tired by mentally tracing the shadow of every venetian-blind slat on her ceiling, when the thought had flown in like a gift: the best way to spy *on* Annie would be to spy *with* Annie.

Spying was solitary work, she reflected as she pulled on the turtleneck sweater she'd chosen for school. Annie had time on her hands, and a good brain. Harriet would draw the girl into her daily routine, and once she had gained Annie's confidence, and access to Morris and Barbara Feigenbaum, the answers to every mystery would be revealed. She picked up her green notebook and tucked it inside the zippered mail pouch she used to disguise it from prying eyes at the Gregory School, then sped down the four flights of stairs to the basement.

"My Lord, what a clatter." Cook looked at her, frowning. "You sound like a whole herd of buffalos."

"Buffalo. Plural and singular."

"Buffalo, plural, if my ears are judging." Cook was slicing a bright red tomato for Harriet's sandwich. There was no need to ask what she wanted for lunch—Harriet had taken a tomato and mayonnaise sandwich to school every day since her sixth birthday. That's half my life, she realized with a shuddering thrill. She reached for a box of cornflakes, upending it into her favorite bowl.

"One of these days, I am not going to find any winter tomatoes worth slicing. Not even at the Koreans'. You'll have to eat ham or bologna like everyone else."

"Should that crisis arise"—Harriet opened the fridge and took out a half-gallon of milk—"I am prepared to go sandwichless. I am not everyone else."

"You can say that again."

Harriet, who secretly enjoyed these exchanges with Cook, opened her mouth. Cook was quicker. "But I hope you won't."

Harriet shrugged and said, "That."

Cook looked blank. "What?"

"I can say 'that' again."

"I can throw a tomato."

"But I hope you won't." Satisfied, Harriet poured the milk into her cornflakes, added a banana, and started to eat.

Cook finished wrapping her sandwich and moved to the sink to rinse off the knife. "Are you going to school with the doctors' niece again?"

Harriet paused, spoon halfway to her mouth. Cook had once made it known that she had had offers of work from the Feigenbaums. Maybe she had inside information. "Why do you ask?" she inquired craftily.

Cook shrugged, tipping her head toward the barred basement window that gave her a view of the neighboring sidewalk. " 'Cause she just left her house."

Harriet leaped to her feet, grabbed her lunch box, and ran, ignoring Cook's frustrated shouts. "Put your bowl in the sink! And don't *clatter*!"

• • •

The sun had come out, and the air was a little bit warmer than the day before. A man chipped away at his snowbound Toyota, and big chunks of ice fell away, crashing into the gutter. "I think doing semaphore letter by letter would take too long," Annie said as they walked down the sidewalk. "Why can't we have signals for whole phrases?"

"Such as?"

Annie thought for a moment. " 'Help, murder!' "

"I don't think that's going to come up."

"It could."

"How about just 'Help'?" said Harriet irritably. "One long flash, one short." She opened her notebook and started to write.

"I've got a better idea," said Annie, stepping into the street. She bent down and picked up two pieces of red plastic that had cracked off someone's taillight. She gave one to Harriet. " 'Help' can be red."

The suggestion did have its dramatic appeal, but Harriet hated to let someone else make the choices. "I've already written *One long and one short*."

"So make that mean something else. Like 'Did you get the homework?' "

She's taking over, thought Harriet. Whose idea was this in the first place? She opened her mouth to protest, but Annie was gazing down at the green notebook.

"What's in there?" she asked.

I've hooked her, thought Harriet. "Nothing," she said in a light, airy voice that implied just the opposite. "Just some notes from my spy route."

"Oh, that," Annie said.

She's feigning disinterest, thought Harriet. I bet she's dying to know. "I'll be making my rounds after school, if you'd like to come with me."

"Why not?" Annie yawned. "I've got nothing better to do."

Harriet shrugged, mirroring Annie's attitude. "If you feel like it."

They had arrived at the steps of the school. Annie turned to face Harriet. "You do understand I can't speak to you if you won't call me Cassandra."

This was outrageous. "I don't see the point."

"It's my name."

"No, it's not."

"At the Gregory School, I'm Cassandra D'Amore." Annie turned and walked straight up the stairs. I'm not going to follow, thought Harriet, folding her arms. And I'm certainly *not* going to call you Cassandra. Enough is enough.

• • •

Annie was good as her word. All day long she refused to respond when anyone, even the gym teacher, addressed her as anything but Cassandra. At lunch, she unwrapped her sandwich—an onion bialy spread with chopped liver—and ate it in silence, while Harriet sat with Beth Ellen and Janie.

"*What's* in that sandwich?" asked Marion Hawthorne, rolling her eyes to the ceiling. "It *smells*."

Annie didn't respond, although Harriet noticed the tips of her ears turning pinker.

I should come to her rescue, she thought, but she didn't say anything.

Marion nudged her friends Carrie and Rachel and stared at Annie's chopped-liver bialy. "I bet someone's hamster is missing this morning." Carrie and Rachel broke into giggles and Marion smirked.

"Don't pick on Cassandra," said Harriet. Annie looked up at her, startled, and then, for the first time, flashed her a genuine smile.

• • •

The girls walked away from school with their backpacks and lunch boxes. "Too much geometry," Harriet groaned. She hated math homework.

"It's nothing," said Annie. "I'll show you some shortcuts. We covered most of it last year at my school in Boston."

"Boston?" said Harriet, suddenly beady-eyed.

Annie took out the cracked piece of red taillight

and squinted through it, closing her other eye. "So what is this spy route about?"

"I watch people," Harriet said, disappointed that Annie had bounced off the subject so quickly. Boston, she thought. Must remember to write that down.

"Who?"

"People with secrets. You know the Dei Santis?"

"The grocery store family?"

Harriet nodded. "They've been on my spy route for over three years. You wouldn't believe all the things I've heard. And Agatha Plumber, the rich one who lives in the mansion right next to the park? I hid in her dumbwaiter once."

"While she was home?" In spite of her mask of disinterest, Annie seemed impressed.

"What would I have to spy on if she wasn't there?" Harriet sounded severe, and reminded herself that her task was to lure Annie into the pleasures of spying. "I've cracked several significant cases," she said, angling her chin for effect.

Annie shrugged. "Okay. Where do we start?"

Victory! thought Harriet, struggling to hide her satisfaction. "Let's go to my house first for cake and milk."

"We did that yesterday."

"I *always* have cake and milk after school."

"Always?"

Harriet nodded, annoyed.

"And you always eat tomato sandwiches?"

"So?"

"You need some variety, Spy Girl." Annie turned to the right.

"My house is that way."

"So?" Annie was mocking her. I do not care for this, Harriet thought as her friend went on. "Let's go around the block. Do something different for once."

"That's ridiculous."

"Is it? I thought you said writers need to experience everything. What's wrong with East Eighty-eighth Street?" It did sound a little absurd, when you looked at it that way. Harriet hesitated, thinking of Cook and her glass of cold milk.

Annie took three more steps and turned back, impatient. "Come on, H'spy, your cake's not going to rot. And who knows, we might find someone awesome to spy on. When my aunt took me to the Koreans' last night, I noticed they've cleared out that vacant lot where the brownstone was knocked down last month. They had shovels and everything. Maybe they're hiding a body."

That did it. Harriet hefted her backpack and set off for East Eighty-eighth Street with Annie, her new-minted partner in spying.

• • •

"There." Annie lifted her arm.

"Don't point, it's too obvious. What am I looking at?"

"Nothing. They've emptied the whole place out. Barrels of garbage. And look." This time she jerked her head to one side without pointing. "What is that truck doing there?"

Inside the chain-link fence was a large, battered box truck, with a couple of planks slanting down to the ground. Harriet narrowed her eyes as a tall, burly man walked out backward, holding one end of a big stack of plywood. He had a few days' growth of beard and his face was unusually red, as if he had scrubbed it with sandpaper. He wore a strange faded hat with long flaps that hung over his ears, giving him the mournful aspect of a basset hound.

As the girls watched, a second man, younger, emerged with the opposite end of the plywood stack, shifting his grip as the older man backed down the planks. "Easy," he said, and the younger man nodded.

"They're building a coffin," whispered Annie.

"Let's stake them out," Harriet said. "Inconspicuously. Have you got any money?"

"I might have some quarters." Annie reached into

her pocket and came up with three. Harriet opened the small zippered pouch on the side of her backpack and took out a dollar bill.

"Excellent. Browse." They strolled to the all-night greengrocers, Happy Fruit Farm, which everyone in the neighborhood called the Koreans'. A clear plastic jacket hung down from the awning, protecting the Granny Smith apples and clementines stacked in neat pyramids outside the shop. The girls situated themselves by a bin of mixed nuts in the shell, which gave them a clear view of the vacant lot and its activities.

"They're father and son," murmured Harriet. "Look at those chins."

Annie nodded. On closer inspection, the man at the back looked no more than sixteen. He had his father's broad shoulders but hadn't grown into his height yet; when he set down the wood, his arms dangled awkwardly. He wore a dull brown quilted vest with an inside-out sweatshirt and threadbare jeans, and his pac boots, which looked way too large, were unlaced. He turned and walked back up the makeshift ramp. So did his father, pausing to hoist up the back of his trousers. Harriet was startled to catch a glimpse of red long johns.

"Where do you think they're from?" she whispered.

Annie whispered back, "Chicago. Gangsters posing as farmers."

I bet they *are* farmers, thought Harriet. She noticed the grocer's wife staring at her, and made a great show of hand-picking just the right mixture of pecans, almonds, walnuts, and hazelnuts. Annie followed her lead without being told. She has an instinct for spying, thought Harriet, pleased to observe that Annie too picked out and threw back the Brazil nuts. "Look at the truck," she said.

Annie turned to weigh her collection of nuts in the hanging scale, giving herself a clearer line of sight. The two men were coming back out with a fresh load of wood. "What about it?" she muttered.

"Those aren't New York license plates," Harriet said, feeling smug that she'd noticed this clue from a distance. "Let's go closer and see where they're from."

"New Hampshire," said Annie, dropping the word's final *r* sound and stretching the vowel in a rather convincing New England accent. Harriet looked at her. Annie shrugged. "State motto 'Live Free or Die.' See 'em all the time."

"In Boston?" Harriet watched closely to see her response.

"There are more in New Hampshire," said Annie. "How about we pay for these nuts and go back home and crack them? My fingers are cold."

"Fine," said Harriet, giving the word a significant

tone. I know why you're changing the subject, she thought. I can wait.

She added her nuts to Annie's and went to the cash register, where Myong-Hee, the languid Korean beauty she often wondered about—was she a relative of the sour owners? An immigrant cousin, perhaps?—was reading a magazine.

"One dollar forty," Myong-Hee said. Harriet paid and went back to give Annie her change. Annie was watching the father and son in the vacant lot. Her eyes lingered on the son as he rolled back a cuff that was missing its button.

"Big hands," she commented. "Both of them. Murderers' hands."

Harriet wished Annie would rein in her imagination and stick to the facts. Spying was not the same thing as fiction. But before she could raise an objection, Annie had grabbed her arm, her voice low and urgent. "We've got to come back here. Tonight."

"My parents won't let me."

"Work out an excuse. You need help with geometry homework, you're coming to my place. It's settled. Meet me right here at eight."

"What if I can't—"

"But you can, H'spy." Annie wheeled on one foot and set off down the block, leaving Harriet speechless.

Harriet looked at the grandfather clock in the library. Fifteen minutes till she was supposed to meet Annie. She'd spread her geometry papers all over the table, letting out such a string of frustrated sighs that her father looked up from his newspaper. "What in the world is the matter?"

"I hate parallelograms," Harriet said. "I can't get them to follow the rules."

"If it makes you feel any better," said Harry Welsch, who worked as a television producer, "I can't even remember the last time I heard the word *parallelogram*. Geometry doesn't come up much in most lines of work."

Harriet's mother was passing along the hall. "I

loved geometry," she said brightly, sticking her head through the door. "Would you like some help?"

That's all I need, Harriet thought. There goes my excuse. Thinking fast, she said, "I'm almost done with my math, but Mrs. LaGoy gave us a biology work sheet that I must have left in my locker. I better call Annie."

"Annie?" said Mrs. Welsch, momentarily puzzled. "Oh, yes, the Feigenbaums' niece. The dramatic one."

"She lives right across the street. I bet I could copy hers."

"Good idea," said Mrs. Welsch. "Ask her to come have some cocoa."

Harriet swallowed hard and said, "Sure." She went to the phone. "Hello, may I speak to Annie?" she said politely.

"Hey, H'spy, who did you think I was?"

"I forgot my biology work sheet," said Harriet, clearing her throat. "And my *mother* thought you could . . . come over with yours?" I hope you can read between the lines, she thought.

"Does that mean you can't make it?" said Annie.

Harriet gulped. Her mother was waiting expectantly. Suddenly inspiration struck. "Oh," she said into the phone, as if Annie had said something entirely different. "So your hair is still wet?"

"What are you talking about?"

"I guess I could go out to *your* house, then." She stole a peek up at her mother, who nodded.

Now Annie caught on. "Good work, H'spy," she said, chuckling. "Meet me at the corner of Second Avenue."

• • •

The air had grown cold and their breath came in clouds. "I can't believe we're doing this," Harriet said. She had smuggled her spy belt and flashlight into her backpack along with her biology book—and, of course, her green notebook.

"You're the one who snuck into some rich lady's dumbwaiter." Harriet chose not to tell Annie that she'd gotten caught. Of all the misfortunes that might befall spies, being caught in action was the most disgraceful. Getting caught in a lie to one's parents was no picnic either.

They rounded the corner of East Eighty-eighth. "Holy Toledo," said Annie. They stared at the vacant lot. In the past several hours, a plywood shack had been erected, just inside the chain-link fence. It was an odd-looking structure—wide and squat, with no windows at all, and a twin row of spikes on the front-facing wall. There were long racks, constructed of two-by-fours, stretching in both directions. The truck with the New Hampshire plates was parked at the back of the lot. Halfway between it and the shack, a small campfire was blazing, with no one in sight.

Annie and Harriet looked at each other. This was far stranger than anything they had imagined. "What is it *for*?" Harriet wondered aloud. "It looks like the jail in some really cheap western."

"I bet they're burning a witch at the stake."

"What stake?"

"They're probably in Central Park, chopping one down."

"Excuse me," drawled someone behind them. They turned at the same time, realizing that they had been blocking the small strip of sidewalk between the parked cars and the brightly lit stacks of fruit, and were shocked to recognize the younger of the two men from New Hampshire. Harriet stared. There were pale flecks of sawdust in his bushy hair. He had wide green eyes and a prominent chin, and he was gripping a pizza box.

"Sure," squeaked Annie, turning scarlet. She scampered between two parked cars, leaving Harriet to draw back against the plastic shield as he carried his pizza box past them and loped toward the campfire.

The door of the shed swung open, and the older

man walked out to meet him, holding a plastic bag with a Happy Fruit Farm logo in one hand and some kind of oddly shaped frame in the other. The girls stood and stared as he set down the bag and unfolded the frame, which turned out to be two canvas camp stools. He sat down on one, reached into the bag, and pulled out two large bottles of root beer. His son sat on the second, opened the pizza box, and handed his father a slice. A few sparks spiraled up from the fire as they sat there and chewed.

"Do you think it's some kind of Satanic ritual?" Annie asked.

"I think it's dinner," said Harriet.

Annie sniffed. "Devil worshippers eat dinner too," she said darkly.

• • •

They agreed to meet ten minutes early for school so that they could walk past the lot with the plywood shack. At Annie's insistence, they didn't ask Sport. "He never *says* anything," she said. "It's creepy."

"Sport isn't creepy. He's shy." Harriet was affronted. She felt the need to defend her best friend.

"Well, he makes *me* feel creepy. Anyway, I think two spies are enough."

There was some logic to this, Harriet had to

concede. They would have to be subtle, especially now that the young man had seen them close up. Two girls heading to the Gregory School with their backpacks were unlikely to catch anyone's eye, but Sport might throw snowballs or something. She wanted to find out what the pizza eaters were planning to do with those weird-looking racks.

"Torture devices, no question," said Annie.

"They're right out in public. The fruit stand is open all night."

"Maybe they're in on it. They own the vacant lot. Maybe they're smuggling drugs in each shipment of kiwifruit. Poisoning your cook's tomatoes."

Maybe not, thought Harriet, but she decided to hold her tongue.

The men were already at work when Annie and Harriet rounded the corner. There were three of them now, two holding the two-by-fours upright as the third swung a sledgehammer.

"I rest my case," Annie whispered, jerking her head toward the shortest man, who was holding one end of the rack. It was the sour-faced Korean grocer.

The man with the hammer made one final pound and laid the tool next to the finished rack. "Ready to unload 'em?" he asked, and the others nodded.

Harriet and Annie exchanged looks. They were probably going to be late for homeroom, but this was too good to miss. Without saying a word, they took up positions in front of the fruit stand, this time pretending to search for the perfect ripe apple.

The three men walked to the truck, the father's gait laid-back and slouching, the son's hulking, the greengrocer's tight and erect. The father and son picked up the long planks that led up to the back of the truck and leaned them in place. With a clatter of metal, the truck's gate rolled up. Both girls stared as the men disappeared into the truck. After a moment or two they heard sounds from inside: indistinct voices, shoving, and a thumping that sounded like something large being lifted.

The son was the first to emerge. Over his shoulder, he carried a giant trussed Christmas tree. His father followed with a second. The grocer was lugging a plump Scotch pine.

"*Christmas* trees," Harriet said, disappointed. "Is that all?" She mentally kicked herself for not recognizing the wooden racks as Christmas tree display stands, even though they were a different shape than the ones the Dei Santis put up every year on the pavement in front of their grocery store. There wasn't a shed at the Dei Santis', either. The Koreans must be trying to corner the market by building a bigger display.

Annie shook her head. "Don't believe it for a second. Those trees are a front."

"You buy?" snapped the grocer's wife, and Harriet realized she had been holding the same apple for several minutes.

"For my teacher," she said with a great show of dignity, hoping she had enough change in her backpack to pay for it.

• • •

Janie Gibbs sat in the lunchroom with Beth Ellen Hansen and three sixth graders, Sara, Amelia, and Alexandra. They were talking about their projects for the school science fair. "I'm going to do one on chemical slime," Sara was saying as Harriet passed them. "You make it with borax and food coloring." Janie looked up at Harriet, patting the last empty seat at their table.

"Oh," said Harriet. "I was planning to sit with Cassandra."

"You never sit with us anymore." Janie's eyes were accusing.

"That's not true," said Harriet. It actually *was* true, but not because she had anything against Janie. She just wanted to spend every ounce of free time trading notes with her co-spy.

For the past several days, she and Annie had followed the same routine. They met ten minutes early and walked to school via the Christmas tree lot; they passed by it again on their way back home. Harriet showed Annie the alley behind the Dei Santis' grocery store, from which they could watch all the intrigues in the stockroom, mostly starring the Dei Santis' rebel son, Fabio, who'd left his fiancée, Marie, for a torrid romance with the dry-cleaner's daughter, Naima. They spied on Harrison Withers, an elderly man whose twenty-six cats had been taken away by the Board of Health (now he was down to a modest nine kittens) and on the Birdlip Twins, the chinless, identically mannered English nannies who worked for the Belgian ambassador.

But their favorite stop on the after-school spy route, by far, was the Christmas tree lot. The racks were now filled with trees, and the pine-needle fragrance was bracing. Wreaths and red-berried garlands hung from the spikes on the front of the shed, in which father and son huddled next to a space heater. Harriet wanted to know everything about these exotically nonurban men, with their wool shirts and earflap hats. Where did they grow their trees? What did they think of New York, with its all-night traffic and Cuban-Chinese diners? Did they actually *sleep* in that shack?

Annie had dubbed the pair Balsam and Douglas

Fir. The girls wondered aloud about wide-eyed Douglas, and why he was spending his days shaking dry needles off trees with a rumbling machine and shoving them through a mechanical hoop that sheathed them in plastic fishnet instead of attending some New Hampshire high school. "He must be a dropout," said Annie with a sniff. "He'll spend the rest of his life hauling carts of manure."

"Maybe he's homeschooled," said Harriet.

Annie shook her head. "Look at him." Douglas was hunched onto one of the camp stools, his unlaced boots splayed out in either direction as he whittled long curls off a piece of wood. "Douglas the Dumbwit."

As for Balsam, the father, he seemed to spend undue amounts of time buying coffee and snacks from Myong-Hee. He would pay her and stand in his checkered wool overshirt, blowing steam off a blue and white cup with a Greek key pattern, trying to come up with something to say. His fingers were weathered and filthy, with battered knuckles. Myong-Hee would pick up her magazine, and after a few awkward moments, Balsam would mumble, "Fine cup of coffee," or, "Well . . . ," and lumber across the street.

"*Nobody* drinks that much coffee," said Harriet sagely. "It's love."

"He's too old," Annie said. "And she doesn't speak English."

"Details," said Harriet.

"Anyway, he must be married to Douglas's mother."

"There's no guarantee of that nowadays." Harriet tried to sound worldly. "Or maybe he's saddled with some mousy farm wife who spends all day knitting and making cheese. He's abandoning her to the acres of stumps while he turns his affections to someone exotic, romantic . . ."

"Disinterested," Annie said. "Myong-Hee doesn't give him the time of day. He brought her a wreath with a red velvet bow, and all she said was 'We Buddhist.' "

"They have to be cautious in front of his son." Harriet knew she was spinning a fantasy—usually Annie's role in their exchanges—but she couldn't stop herself. "Maybe Balsam was tragically widowed."

"Or just plain divorced. Like my parents will be any minute," Annie said bitterly. Harriet stared at her. So *that* was why Annie was staying at her aunt and uncle's. What else was she going to confess? Would her secrets gush out in a flood? Harriet wasn't sure how to proceed. If she said the wrong thing, Annie might slam on the lid, and they'd be right back where they started. But something else stopped her from speaking. She had never seen Annie emotional, and now, Harriet noticed, there were tears just behind her friend's lashes. Not knowing what else to do, she reached out and laid her hand awkwardly on Annie's arm.

"Get your fingerless gloves off me, H'spy." Annie's voice sounded sharp, as if she were embarrassed and trying to hide it. "I've had it with watching these dumbwits. Let's go eat some cake."

CHAPTER 4

Sport stared at the long list of deli meats over the counter at Dei Santi's Market. "What does she bring for lunch?"

"Who?" said Harriet irritably, though she knew full well there was only one "she" on Sport's mind these days.

"Yolanda." Sport's voice went from tenor to bass and back.

Harriet put her hand up to one ear and adopted the nasal twang of a phone operator. "I'm sorry, there's no listing for that name—"

"All right, all right, *Annie*. What kind of bread does she use for her sandwiches? White, whole wheat, rye?"

"There's no pattern," said Harriet. "Her aunt doesn't have a clue what goes into a school lunch. Today she had leftover Chinese takeout and a corn muffin."

Sport made a face. Behind the counter, Papa Dei Santi straightened his apron and pulled on the string that flipped over the customer numbers. "Eighty-six," he mumbled.

"That's me," said Sport, moving up eagerly. Harriet watched as he took out a much-folded grocery list. Sport had a stepmother now, but he'd shopped for his father for so many years that he still considered it his job, not Kate's. Kate, whose office was way across town, was only too happy to let Sport take charge, and Sport's father, Matthew, couldn't have cared less if anyone *ever* bought groceries, as long as he had enough coffee to stay up and work on his novel all night.

Harriet wondered how Matthew and Kate had figured out they were in love. Had it been an instantaneous realization, as Sport claimed he'd had when the girl with green shoes had picked up his pencil? One minute he was his normal self; the next he was head over heels in love.

Harriet found the whole subject absurd. She'd picked up plenty of boys' pencils and it hadn't changed her life one bit. The phrase "falling in love" seemed morbidly apt: Sport made it sound unexpected, sudden, and possibly fatal, like falling into a manhole while crossing the street. The boy who was standing in front of her, asking Papa Dei Santi to slice the Virginia ham thinner, was not the same Sport who had been her best friend since preschool.

Oh well, she thought, I have a new best friend anyway. Luckily Annie had not fallen victim to Sport's disease. She thought Sport was a bore and love was a waste of emotion; the week before, when a cold snap had forced the girls indoors to spend an afternoon spying on patients of both Drs. Feigenbaum, she had told Harriet that living with a gynecologist *and* a psychiatrist had turned her off romance for life.

None of their classmates agreed. The Gregory School was coed through sixth grade, and it seemed to Harriet that boys had been banished in the nick of time: all the seventh-grade girls were obsessed with them. Even Janie, the no-nonsense chemist, had left common sense behind, mooning over a pop star named Jason Orlando, whose breathy voice sounded to Harriet's ears like a calf with its foot in a trap. Janie's locker was plastered with teen magazine photos; she'd even moved some of her chemistry things from her bedroom to install a new stereo system and life-size fan poster. She talked about Jason nonstop.

"Why do you keep calling him by his first name? You don't even *know* him," Harriet snapped as they tied their sneakers for gym class.

Janie rolled her eyes and shot her a don't-you-know-*anything* look. "Yes, I do."

"Well, he doesn't know *you*."

"That's his loss," said Janie. "And anyway, that's just a detail. When Jason does meet me, he'll fall in love in a nanosecond. Spontaneous combustion."

Harriet tied her lace in a triple knot. She thought about making a cutting comeback, but she was too irritated to come up with anything witty. It's one thing for Marion Hawthorne and the popularity clones to have idiot crushes, but if this can happen to *Janie*, thought Harriet darkly, it can happen to anyone. Even to me.

Annie had stayed home from school that day—she'd been fighting a cold, and her aunt was a world-class worrier—so Harriet left school alone. She thought about taking the usual detour to spy on the Christmas tree men, but the thought of a thin slice of Cook's lemon pound cake and a glass of cold milk sitting inside the fridge, on the same shelf where Cook left her afternoon snack every day, was too irresistible. She headed for East Eighty-seventh Street.

Cook had gone home early, as she always did on

Fridays, leaving a casserole covered in plastic wrap and a pot of soup next to Harriet's cake and milk. Both pots had taped-on reheating instructions in Cook's solid block letters. I wonder if she minds, Harriet thought as she chewed her pound cake, which was not lemon, but marble. I wonder if she gets sick of making a dinner for us every Friday and then taking the subway to Brooklyn and making another for her lazy son. *I'd* mind.

Harriet stared out the basement window at the Feigenbaums' nearly identical window across the street, wondering if Annie's aunt had forced her to stay in bed all day long. She felt strangely restless. I'm not used to being alone anymore, she realized. For years she had come home from school, eaten her cake, and spent the afternoon spying and then visiting with her beloved Ole Golly. When Ole Golly left to get married, Harriet had added new stops to her spy route to fill in the gap. She'd taken to making long phone calls to Sport, or visiting him in his walk-up apartment, on those too-frequent nights when her parents went out, her mother adrift in a swath of silk scarves and Chanel N°5 and her father adjusting his glasses, which always sat on a different slant than the bow tie he wore with his tux. She'd discovered the luxurious thrill of having the house to herself after dark. More time to write, she had exulted, with no interruptions.

But all that had changed when Annie moved in. Now Harriet went through her daily spy route with a talkative sidekick. The silence that once had felt special and rich now felt empty. I'm *bored*, she thought with amazement, turning over a concept that had never seemed to apply to her. I'm lonely and bored.

She set her cake plate and fork in the sink. There was no point in calling anyone else: she'd just get stuck listening to Janie rave about Jason or Sport lose his brains for Yolanda. How does this *happen* to people? she wondered.

Harriet headed upstairs and took out a green notebook. Her last entries were sparse, and she realized she'd spent more time speculating aloud with Annie than taking notes. This would not do. Ole Golly had always impressed on her that writers needed to experience everything and to write it all down. "Isaac Bashevis Singer said, 'God gave us so many emotions, and so many strong ones. Every human being, even if he is an idiot, is a millionaire in emotions.' " Ole Golly had paused to make sure that Harriet took in her words. "The difference between one millionaire and another, between writers and everyone else, is merely a matter of pen and ink."

Harriet picked up her pen and stared at her green

notebook, frowning. She didn't feel much like a millionaire. Everyone *else* is having emotions, she thought, even if they're really stupid ones. Nothing is happening to *me*.

All right, then write about that, she thought. Ole Golly told me to write about everything. She thought for a moment, then set pen to paper.

WHY DO PEOPLE HAVE CRUSHES? AND WHO CAME UP WITH THAT WORD FOR IT, ANYWAY? "CRUSH" SOUNDS LIKE SOMETHING THAT HAPPENS TO WINDSHIELDS IN CAR CRASHES. IS IT BECAUSE PEOPLE ACT CRACKED WHEN THEY HAVE THEM? WHAT MAKES PEOPLE THINK THEY'RE IN LOVE?

An inspiration struck her. Ole Golly will know, she thought. In the course of the past year, Ole Golly had fallen in love with George Waldenstein, married him, moved up to Montreal, left him with plans to expunge him forever from memory, and had a dramatic reunion. She was expecting his baby in just a few months. Ole Golly must be a billionaire in emotions, thought Harriet. She's a tycoon.

She dug through her desk drawer and hauled out the present Ole Golly had given her last Christmas, an elegant box of stationery from her favorite store, Jasmine's Art Supply, with textured paper and cream-colored envelopes tied with a pale satin ribbon.

Harriet carried it into the butter yellow bedroom across the hall, where Ole Golly had slept when she lived there. She sat down at the writing desk under a framed print of Van Gogh's *Sunflowers* and snapped on the sensible desk lamp. The afternoon hours no longer stretched ahead forlorn and empty. I know just what to do with myself, she gloated. I'll write to Ole Golly.

• • •

By bedtime, the wastebasket overflowed with wadded-up cream-colored paper. When Harriet finally finished a version she liked, she looked at the clock on her dresser and realized that, for the first time, she was late for her nine-thirty flashlit goodnight.

"Where were you?" demanded Annie the following morning. "I semaphored *twice*."

"Important international correspondence," said Harriet, tapping the envelope on which she had written AIR MAIL, PAR AVION, and VIA AEREA, just in case.

"Fancy schmantzy," said Annie. "I suppose that explains your neglecting an ailing friend?"

"I forgot, okay?" Harriet strode to the corner mailbox and dropped in her letter. "Anyway, you're all better."

"I was never that sick in the first place." Annie shrugged. "My aunt Barbara's a lunatic. Anything new on the spy route?"

"Nothing of note." Harriet was reluctant to admit she'd gone straight home for cake and milk.

"Let's stake out the premises after school. I have a feeling the case is about to break open. A turf war with the Dei Santis." Annie spotted a soda can on the sidewalk and kicked it into the snowbank. Harriet chased her, relieved to find someone her age who still wanted to be a kid.

• • •

"With love's light wings did I o'erperch these walls;
For stony limits cannot hold love out:
And what love can do, that dares love attempt;
Therefore thy kinsmen are no stop to me."

Mr. Grenville held the textbook away from his face and intoned like an actor, even though, with his thinning hair combed over and sprayed in a mat, he was nobody's picture of Romeo. All across the classroom, girls leaned over their desks with their cheeks propped on their palms, looking dreamy-eyed. Janie was actually stroking the photo of Jason Orlando on the key chain that hung from her purse.

Harriet stifled a giggle. She glanced back at Annie, who pointed at Janie and rolled her eyes. Harriet smiled.

When the bell rang at three, they were first down the steps. "We need to come up with a cover," said Harriet as they walked side by side toward the Christmas tree stand. "We can't just keep hanging around the Koreans'. If we pick up any more fruit without buying it, Mrs. Kim's going to boil us in oil."

Annie thought for a moment. "We could build a snowman," she said. "Right there, on the edge of the fence. That would give us a clear line of sight."

"Too suspicious."

"We're kids! Kids all over the world build snowmen. Well, maybe not in Borneo."

Harriet shook her head. "It would call too much attention to us. Anyway, the snow is disgusting."

Annie looked down at the curb. It was true. The last snowfall had been on the ground for so long that the drifts were black-edged and grainy with soot. "I know!" she said, a triumphant smile blazing across her face. "Let's shop for a Christmas tree!"

"What?" Harriet stopped in her tracks, staring at Annie as if she'd gone crazy. "Is that what you call undercover?"

"It's deep undercover. It's hiding in plain sight. Don't you see? We've walked past the stand and hung around staring a million times, but we've never been inside the fence. If we go in as customers, they won't be suspicious at *all*. We can get up close and personal." Annie's eyes were shining.

"But it doesn't make sense," argued Harriet. "The worst thing a spy can do is to let someone make her. That means 'identify,' " she added importantly.

"Nonsense," said Annie. "The worst thing a spy can do is to pass up a great opportunity. We might even get to see inside the shed, where Douglas and Balsam keep their stuff. Where their *secrets* are. What are you waiting for?"

Harriet knew it was useless to argue. "Wreaths," she said, nodding. "They're on the shed wall."

"Good thinking, H'spy." Annie grinned and set off.

• • •

Douglas was sprawled on a stool with his legs splayed out, leaning his broad back against the fence. He had something clutched in his lap, and his lips moved a bit as he peered at it, turning a page. "Look," Annie whispered. "The Dumbwit is reading a *book*." Douglas looked up and she reddened.

"Can I help you with something?" His voice was woolly and low, with a slight scratchy drawl that made it dead clear he was *not* from the city.

"Um, wreaths?" Annie's voice had gone squeaky again.

"We're just looking," said Harriet breezily, hoping to cover for her friend's sudden nervousness. "My mom will come back here to pay for one later."

"Be my guest," Douglas nodded. "I'm here if you got any questions."

Annie nodded, mute, scuttling to the far end of the shed, which was studded with twin rows of wreaths. She pretended to look at a huge white pine wreath, braided with holly and tied with a shiny gold ribbon. "How about this one?"

"Too big," said Harriet loudly, striding her way. "That's for a lobby or something." She stood next to Annie and fingered a smaller wreath, flipping the price tag. "Science fiction," she said in a sidelong whisper. Annie looked blank.

"What he's *reading*," Harriet told her impatiently. "*The Chronicles of* something or other. Douglas's thumb was on top of the word. His nails are incredibly grimy."

This last observation pleased her no end. Attention to detail was the essence of spying; one never knew what might turn out to be crucial.

"Science fiction," said Annie, dripping disdain. "That figures."

She glanced at Douglas, whose back was to them. He turned a page, lost in his reading. "Let's look inside the shed before Balsam gets back."

Harriet frowned, looking at Douglas. "But . . ."

"He won't even notice, he's somewhere on Pluto. Come on, you're a spy." She reached forward and pushed the door open. Harriet winced as the hinges creaked. Inside the windowless shed they could make out two cots heaped with blankets and sleeping bags, a landslide of discarded clothing and take-out containers, a pair of old boots. "What's that smell?" Annie whispered.

A figure sat up on the cot, pushing aside the open newspaper that covered his face. It was Balsam, in faded and coffee-stained long johns. "Private back here," he said mildly. "Do I go into *your* living quarters? My very word."

• • •

"That was *awful*," said Harriet. Her heart was still pounding.

"Balsam didn't know we were spying. He just thought we'd made a mistake."

"We did. An enormous mistake. We can't ever go back there again."

"You worry too much, H'spy," Annie said. She

climbed down from her stool at the Feigenbaums' kitchen counter and went to the stove, taking off the white kettle before it shrilled. She poured steaming water into two mugs and opened a packet of cocoa. "It's diet. That's all they have."

"Any marshmallows?"

"Dream on. There might be some high-fiber Ry-Krisp or something." She opened the fridge. "Do you like chopped liver? I hate it."

Barbara Feigenbaum entered the kitchen, her large earrings clunking against her neck. She was tanned even in winter, with close-cropped and lacquered black hair. Her shoulders hunched slightly, giving her the look of a beady-eyed bird. "Oh good, you girls found a snack. Do you have any homework?"

Annie shrugged. "Couple of work sheets."

"And act three of *Romeo and Juliet*," Harriet reminded her.

"Shakespeare," said Barbara, taking a bottle of seltzer and drifting back out. "Very nice."

Annie took the book out of her backpack, holding it at arm's length. She flopped her hair over one side of her head and intoned, "*If love be rough with you, be rough with love; Prick love for pricking, and you beat love down.*"

Harriet peered at her. "What do you think about crushes?"

"Ridiculous."

"Pointless."

"Childish."

Harriet was vastly relieved. "I don't understand all these girls turning suddenly stupid and going around telling everyone they're in love."

"In love is not the same thing as a *crush*." Annie landed on the last word with a sneer of disdain, but something had changed in her voice.

Harriet stared at her. "Annie?"

"What?" Annie's tone was offhand, but her cheeks had a definite flush.

"Are you trying to tell me you've fallen in love?"

"Of course not," said Annie, turning as red as a beefsteak tomato.

"Who is he?" Harriet's tone was demanding.

Annie paused, then lifted a hand to her forehead like the star of a Hollywood film. Her voice was Cassandra D'Amore's. "I'm not at liberty to say."

"I don't believe this. What's *wrong* with you?"

"Nothing is wrong, H'spy, I'm a woman in love. With an older man."

Harriet stared. "It's not Mr. Grenville, is it?"

"Yuck!" Annie opened her mouth, pointing down at her tongue in a vomiting gesture. "That's revolting!"

"Then *who*?" Harriet practically screamed.

"I have a right to my secrets." Annie picked up her cocoa and gulped.

Not from me, thought Harriet, watching through narrowed eyes. Not from your best friend. And certainly not from a spy.

When Morris Feigenbaum's last patient left for the day, Harriet headed back home. She opened the heavy front door and looked at the tray on the sideboard where the maid always left the day's mail. There was nothing of interest, just a phone bill, an L.L. Bean catalog, and a *New Yorker* magazine full of cartoons about rich people's parties. No letters from Montreal. Somebody has to explain this to me, thought Harriet. It had been bad enough to lose Janie and Sport to the ranks of the mushy deluded, but Annie's declaring that she was in love was the last straw. There's nobody left, thought Harriet, flopping down on her belly on the couch. I'm the last bastion of sanity.

"Harry? Is that you?" Harriet's mother came into the library wearing an evening dress, her head tilted to one side as she put on an earring.

"It's me," said Harriet, prone.

"Oh, hi, darling. I thought you were over at Annie's."

"I'm back."

"That's nice." Her mother sounded distracted. "Your father is late, for a change. We're supposed to go out with the Connellys, and he simply can't wear his suit. It's a black-tie reception. I bet he's forgotten."

"I haven't." Her father's voice boomed through the doorway. "Though if I had the knack of forgetting an evening with Sylvia Connelly, I'd be a happier man."

He leaned down to kiss Harriet's cheek. "You look like you're swimming indoors. I hope that's not preadolescent moping I see."

"No, Daddy."

"Good. That would make me feel old." Perhaps because Harriet's father worked in television, it seemed to her sometimes that he had a permanent layer of sarcasm.

"Harry, you *have* to get dressed," said her mother.

"I know, I know. Can't a man say hello to his daughter?"

"You're going out again?" said Harriet.

"Yes dear," her mother answered. "You're staying here and Cook will be staying too. I left you our number."

"We won't need to call you!" Harriet exclaimed. "I can fend for myself." She picked up a pillow and headed upstairs, stamping loudly on each stair tread.

She unlocked the old toy box at the foot of her bed and took out her green notebook. As always, the sight of the volumes arrayed in numerical order gave her a ripple of pride. Ole Golly had called the green notebooks Harriet's *oeuvre*, which was a French word for "body of work." My oeuvre looks pretty substantial, thought Harriet, running a hand along the books' spines. She felt better already. She picked up her favorite pen, the one with the peacock blue ink in a small plastic cartridge, and started to write.

ANNIE SMITH CLAIMS SHE'S IN LOVE WITH AN OLDER MAN. I HAVE WITNESSED NO EVIDENCE. COULD SHE BE FAKING IT?

Harriet paused for a minute, then wrote, WHY?

It didn't seem logical that she would lie. To be sure, Annie had invented a long list of phony identities, but none of her names had been secret. The fact that she wouldn't identify her older man gave the phantom some weight.

CLUES AND POSSIBLE SUSPECTS, she wrote, and paused again before writing, NOT MR. GRENVILLE.

It wasn't a whole lot to go on. There was only one other male teacher at the Gregory School, Mr. Bolbach, and he was a wheezing antique with ill-fitting false teeth. Maybe it's somebody I haven't met yet, she thought. This older man might be a teacher from Annie's old school, or even an eighth or ninth grader. He might be a friend of Sport's.

INTERROGATE SPORT, she wrote, and the instant the words were on paper, she knew what she wanted to do. She closed her notebook, locked it back in the trunk, and ran down the stairs to her parents' room. Her father was grumbling his way into a stiff white shirt. Mrs. Welsch sat at her vanity, brushing on blush. Harriet could see three of her mother in the angled mirrors, and all of them looked very elegant.

"Can I go to Sport's place for dinner?" Harriet panted.

Mrs. Welsch turned, one cheek deep rose and the other still pale. She looked at her husband as if for permission and said, "I suppose. . . ."

"Thanks!" exclaimed Harriet, and clattered upstairs before they had a chance to discuss it. She grabbed hold of the phone in the upstairs hall, twining its long cord around her hand as she placed a call to a number she knew by heart.

• • •

Sport and Kate were making a big pot of two-alarm chili, a favorite from back in the days when Sport had to fix his dad dinners of rice, beans, and pasta six days out of seven. It was still Matthew's favorite, though Kate had upgraded the recipe with big chunks of beef browned in onions and olive oil.

"Texans never use hamburger meat," she told Harriet, who was helping her chop the cilantro. "It's chunk beef or chicken, or if you want to be really authentic, roadkill armadillo." Kate's ex-husband was from Lubbock, so she was a fount of such lore.

Harriet always enjoyed eating dinner at Sport's. The kitchen was cozy, and Kate and Sport elbowed each other good-naturedly, jostling for counter space. Matthew never emerged from his desk till the food hit the table. He still used an old-fashioned typewriter that dinged at the end of each line, and the pauses and bursts of staccato behind his closed door were a comforting sound track to life at the Rocques'. He's a *real* writer, thought Harriet, admiring the audible rhythms of Matthew's new novel. Sport arched to one side, still circling his spoon in the chili pot, as Kate opened the oven and took out a skillet of corn bread.

• • •

"Better than ever." Matthew beamed, leaning back on two legs of his chair with his hands splayed out over his stomach. "Who wants some ice cream?"

"You finished the ice cream last night," said Sport.

"I did?"

"Around three in the morning," said Kate, scraping plates. "You told me it gave you a second wind."

"I forgot about that. What a crime. You've got to have ice cream with chili."

Harriet looked at Sport. She'd been hoping to catch him alone; it didn't do to interrogate people in front of two witnesses. "Why don't we go to the deli and pick some up?"

"Excellent," Matthew said. "I vote for coffee."

Sport frowned. "It's my turn to do dishes."

"I've got 'em," Kate said. "You two scat."

• • •

Harriet waited till Sport had bought two quarts of ice cream, one coffee, one butter pecan, before popping the question. "Who did Yolanda like at your school?"

"Like?" Sport turned. "You mean *like* like, or—"

"Crush. Did you ever notice her looking at anyone that way? He might have been older," she added offhandedly.

Sport shook his head. "I would have punched the guy right in the nose." He put change in his pocket and picked up the bag. "Does she still wear those green shoes?" he asked in a reverent tone.

Harriet groaned inwardly. I'm in for it now, she thought. I brought up the subject, and now I'll be stuck with it. "Waterproof boots," she said, shaking her head.

"Boots," echoed Sport in a dreamy voice.

I don't get this at *all*, thought Harriet. They've all gone wacko.

• • •

After they ate their ice cream, Harriet helped Kate dry the dishes while Sport and his dad watched a hockey game on TV. She looked at the wedding band shining on Kate's left hand. Maybe she can explain this in-love stuff, Harriet thought. Kate and Matthew are newlyweds, just like Ole Golly and Mr. Waldenstein.

"Kate?" she asked.

"What?" Kate stretched up to stack bowls in a cabinet.

"How did you first fall in love?"

Kate looked at her, eyebrows arched. "With Matthew, you mean? Or when I was sixteen?"

"Either. Both."

"Well," Kate said thoughtfully, "it's kind of like running a fever. You don't always know when it starts, but at some point you realize that you're unusually warm. Does that make any sense?"

"I guess," said Harriet, sounding unsure.

Kate smiled. "Is he someone you know?" she asked gently.

"Who?"

"You don't have to tell me," said Kate. Her eyes twinkled. "Sometimes it's more fun to keep it a secret. Especially if he's a friend."

Harriet stared at her. "You don't think that I—"

"No, of course not," said Kate, just a little too quickly. Her voice was amused.

"I wouldn't be caught *dead*," said Harriet, so loudly that Matthew and Sport turned from the hockey game to stare at her.

• • •

Harriet stood in the bathroom, brushing her teeth till the toothpaste foamed. She spit into the sink. How could Kate even think such a thing? The idea that

Harriet M. Welsch, writer and spy, would develop a crush on *anyone*, much less on Sport, was appalling. Sport was her *friend*.

True, he had changed a lot in the last year, and not just because of his crush on some fake name of Annie's. He'd gone through a growth spurt that had suddenly made him a head taller than Harriet, so her gaze fell between Sport's lumpy Adam's apple and his wispy-haired chin. His manner was different too: gruffer, as if he were trying to fit with the older, more streetwise boys on his new baseball team. He still enjoyed cooking, but he no longer talked about cleansers and recipes without any self-consciousness the way he had back in the days before Kate had moved in. If somebody thought it was weird that Sport cooked and cleaned for his father, well, that was *their* problem.

He wants to be normal, she thought, shutting off the cold-water tap. What a weird thing to want.

• • •

She watched Annie closely for clues throughout the next day. As Cassandra D'Amore, making dramatic pronouncements to classmates, she might leak some key information. But Cassandra confined herself to a few airy glosses on *Romeo and Juliet*, vis-à-vis "certain occurrences witnessed at family events in my previous walk of life." Mr. Grenville seized on the chance to paint the Montagues and Capulets as rival Mafia families or street gangs and even broke into a couple of bars of the Jet song from *West Side Story*.

Annie wanted to walk past the Christmas tree stand after school. Harriet thought they should lie low for a while. "We were in their *bedroom*," she said. "There's no way we can do any serious spying."

Annie rolled her eyes. "You're so predictable."

"Let's check on the rest of the route. It's been eons since we watched the Birdlip Twins. And what about Fabio and Naima?"

"They kiss too much."

"True. And he smokes besides. Wouldn't he taste like a furnace?"

"I wouldn't know," Annie said primly. "I'd never consider a smoker."

Nonsmoker, thought Harriet. Might be a clue.

In the end they decided to spy on the Birdlips. The Belgian embassy was a narrow white building with several flags. There was a strip of reserved parking at the curb, which usually boasted a town car or two with red, white, and blue diplomatic license plates. Sometimes drivers lounged in their front seats, wearing brimmed hats or dark sunglasses, listening to foreign radio stations.

The ambassador and his wife had a ground-floor apartment next to the embassy building. They had three young children, a toddler girl and twin infants, and not one but two English nannies. The Birdlip Twins weren't actual twins—they might not have even been sisters—but they were both pale and chinless and moved with an eerie sameness, like synchronized swimmers. Even their names were close to identical: Maggie and Megan. When Harriet spotted the pair of them wheeling twin strollers through the pathways of Carl Schurz Park, she had tailed them back home to the embassy and added them to her spy route.

The Birdlips shared a bedroom/sitting room just off the nursery, whose tall casement windows made warm-weather spying a cinch. But today all the windows were closed, and Annie and Harriet couldn't hear anything. They quickly got tired of watching Maggie and Megan sort toddler socks into pairs and stack diapers. "Let's check in on Harrison and his nine kittens," said Harriet. "They must be getting big."

"My fingers are freezing," said Annie. "Let's check in on cocoa."

"How about tomorrow?" said Harriet, watching her closely. "Have you got any plans for the weekend?"

"Um, I'm free on Sunday." Annie turned her head, watching a pigeon soar skyward. She's hiding something, thought Harriet.

"What are you doing tomorrow?" she pressed.

Annie's eyes stayed on the pigeon as it landed on top of a row of brick chimneys on one of the neighboring buildings. "I wonder if that's where they nest."

"Something with your aunt and uncle?"

Annie's nod looked a little too grateful. "Aunt Barbara insisted. It's some kind of Hanukkah thingy they do at their temple."

"You celebrate Hanukkah?" Harriet asked, surprised. Smith didn't sound very Jewish, though now that she thought of it, Feigenbaum did. Was Annie Smith's "real" name fake, then?

"My mother is Jewish, my dad grew up Methodist. We kind of made up our own blend: Christmas tree and menorah, latkes with Easter eggs. Aunt Barbara and Uncle Morris never approved. I guess now it's their chance to straighten me out."

This was far more than Annie had ever told Harriet about her family, but Harriet couldn't help thinking that something was off. Her friend hadn't met her eyes yet.

"What time is this temple thing done? We could meet after that."

Annie flushed. "I don't know exactly. I'll call you."

Bingo, thought Harriet. Caught you.

• • •

The next morning, Harriet rushed through her breakfast and took a position right next to the living room window, where she could watch the Feigenbaums' house through the slats of the blind without being seen from the street. She held an open copy of *Romeo and Juliet* in her lap, in case her parents happened to wonder why she was glued to the beige brocade wing chair. Her spy belt, flashlight, and notebook were in her school backpack. An outgrown ski parka that Annie had never seen hung within easy reach, along with a pair of lensless glasses frames she kept on hand as a disguise. Stakeouts were dull, but Harriet relished the heightened sense of awareness that came with a long observation. She passed the time by trying to come up with the right succinct phrase for every person who walked down the sidewalk: a jogger with legs like a greyhound; a flat-footed West Indian nanny waddling after a plastic-swathed stroller.

It was almost eleven a.m. when the Feigenbaums' door finally opened. Harriet straightened at once. She peered through the blind slats as Morris, wrapped in a bulky tweed coat and Russian-style rabbit-fur hat, held the door open for Barbara, whose wide-belted trenchcoat made her look even tinier than usual. Then he turned back and locked the front door with a key. They walked down the stoop arm in arm. Annie was nowhere in sight. I knew it, thought Harriet, feeling triumphant. She looked at her wristwatch. I give her five minutes, she thought. As soon as they're out of range.

A short-haired blond woman with two springer spaniels walked past, but Harriet couldn't be bothered with finding apt phrases. She pulled on the navy blue parka, shouldered her backpack, and stared at the Feigenbaums' door. Six minutes passed. Then she saw something move in the alley alongside the brownstone, where they kept the trash cans, and caught a quick glimpse of a red beret.

Annie looked up and down as she opened the wooden gate, letting herself onto East Eighty-seventh Street. Harriet froze, holding her breath, even though she knew full well there was no way she could be spotted behind the closed blinds. She waited till she could see Annie's back heading west. Then she put on her glasses frames, pulled up the hood of her parka, and slipped out the door.

CHAPTER 6

Harriet stayed on the shady side of the street, keeping her distance from Annie. Even with her unfamiliar ski parka zipped up to her nose, she was careful to alter her walk so that she wouldn't be recognized if Annie happened to glance her way. She was grateful that Annie had worn her bright red beret—it would be hard to lose sight of, even in the crush of holiday shoppers along Eighty-sixth Street, the neighborhood thoroughfare.

Annie went west along Eighty-sixth till she got to Third Avenue. After crossing, she paused at the corner, took a deep breath, and entered a brightly lit, glass-fronted stand with giant signs trumpeting

PAPAYA KING—FRESH JUICES—HOT DOGS. Harriet crossed the street quickly, before the light changed, and positioned herself right outside the big window, where she'd be obscured by a *Drink to Your Health!* poster.

There was no place to sit, just a take-out counter and high, round tables where people could rest their cardboard trays while they ate standing up. There were several customers sipping juice drinks out of tall yellow cups. One of them smiled, dropped his empty cup into the garbage, and went to meet Annie.

Harriet stared. He was older, all right—he appeared to be in his mid-twenties. He was dressed in a handwoven jacket that looked Guatemalan, and wore his blond hair hanging over his collar. He even had sort of a beard, a small goatee patch beneath his lower lip. He looks like an off-season surfer, thought Harriet.

What happened next startled her even more. The window glass muffled the sound, but she clearly saw the blond surfer type mouth the word "Annie?" as if he were asking a question. When she nodded, he held out his hand (woven hemp watchband on right wrist; attention to detail) and shook Annie's hand. It seemed they were meeting each other for the first time. I don't get it, thought Harriet. Did she fall in love with an older-man pen pal?

Before she could wonder too long, she realized Annie was turning in her direction. Harriet dipped her head lower, pretending to read the small print on a price list, and let them walk past her. The surfer guy's words drifted to her ear as they went through the door.

". . . didn't want you to take any chances," he was saying to Annie.

Chances? thought Harriet. What kind of chances?

"So I'll bring you right down to the restaurant," he finished. Annie nodded, her hands jammed down deep in her pockets, her shoulders held rigid.

They walked up the sidewalk to Lexington Avenue. Harriet didn't dare to stay close enough to overhear what they said, but the blond guy seemed to be doing the bulk of the talking. When they got to the corner, he craned his head uptown and Harriet heard him say, "Perfect. There's our bus."

Not so perfect for *me*, thought Harriet. She couldn't very well get on the same bus—Annie would certainly recognize her in so close a space—and she wouldn't be able to keep up on foot. Nor had she brought enough cash for a cab, even if she'd been willing to wheedle the driver into stopping at every bus stop and waiting.

Harriet scanned the bus as it pulled to the curb and opened its doors with a pneumatic hiss. Every window was jam-packed with passengers standing back to back in the aisle. There was plenty of traffic on Lexington. With all these holiday shoppers forcing the bus to stop every two blocks, Harriet might stand a chance if Annie wasn't going far. What do I have to lose? she thought.

She crossed Eighty-sixth Street and started downtown at a racewalker's clip. It would take a few minutes for that long bus line to file on board; she could get a jump start. The bus overtook her at Eighty-fourth, but sure enough, four people were waiting at the next stop, and the bus groaned its way to the curb to make room for them.

Harriet kept pace for twelve more blocks, first getting ahead of the bus, then nearly losing it, then barely catching up at the next stop. The navy blue parka was making her sweat, and she longed to unzip it. I hope they're not going much farther downtown, she thought. I need a breather.

As if in answer, the surfer and Annie got off the bus just below Seventy-second Street. Annie glanced around nervously, touching her red beret. Harriet stepped to the side of a newsstand just in the nick of time, hiding behind magazine racks and cheap winter scarves. "Ready?" she heard the man say. Annie mumbled something she couldn't make out. He patted her shoulder—not, in Harriet's rather inexpert opinion, the way a boyfriend would touch her—and opened the door of a seafood restaurant with dark wooden columns and elegant tablecloths.

Harriet sidled up to the window's far corner. Facing the street, she craned her neck over her shoulder to look inside. A uniformed headwaiter stood at his station, arching his eyebrows expectantly. A tall man with curly brown hair got up from the bar and went straight to them, pumping the surfer guy's hand and stepping back to look at Annie. He opened his arms and she went to him dutifully, letting him fold her into an embrace.

Harriet practically screamed with shock. The first guy was old, but this one was older—a bona fide grown-up, nearly her parents' age, his sandy curls starting to thin at the temples. Had Annie gone out of her mind?

The two men were talking now, and the younger one nodded and laughed. He went over to sit on the older one's barstool, raising his hand to signal the bartender. The older man turned to Annie with a broad smile, which she returned awkwardly. He led her over to the headwaiter, who looked in his reservation book, nodded, and brought them inside.

Annie took off her coat and beret and laid them on the green leather seat of a private banquette. Harriet's view of the man was obscured by the curve of the bench—she could see just the top of his curly head—but she had a clear angle on Annie, who seemed to be, uncharacteristically, at a loss for words. She glanced at the bar, where the younger man had taken off his woven jacket and gotten a Bloody Mary.

Harriet's imagination had gone into overdrive. Why would Annie go out to lunch with a man more than twice her age, and who was that guy at the bar? A bodyguard trying to pass himself off as a surfer dude? Why would the older man *need* a bodyguard? Maybe Annie was pulling a double cross, pretending to lie but actually telling the truth when "Cassandra" dropped all those dark hints about the Witness Protection Program. Maybe the Feigenbaums weren't really her uncle and aunt but Mafia hit men maintaining an unlikely cover as Upper East Side Jewish doctors.

The headwaiter had returned to his station and was glaring indignantly at the girl whose nose was now pressed to his window. Harriet took a step back and realized that the turbaned Sikh at the corner newsstand was staring at her as well. I need a cover myself, she thought.

She looked up and down the block and fixed on a Greek coffee shop on the opposite corner. There was a row of small tables along the front window, just right for a stakeout. Harriet went to the crosswalk and waited as cabs and delivery vans inched down the crowded street. Someone was playing a radio so loudly that she could feel the bass throbbing through the closed windows: a rock 'n' roll version of "Silent Night."

• • •

The Greek waitress gave Harriet the evil eye every time she passed, even though Harriet was a legitimate paying customer. True, she had bought only one Coke and had sat at this table for more than an hour, scrawling notes in her notebook and looking up sharply whenever the door of the seafood restaurant swung open, but there was no law against drinking your soda too slowly.

A balding waiter slouched by with a tray full of sizzling shish kebabs that smelled richly of garlic, and Harriet realized she had skipped lunch. She wished she'd brought more than a couple of dollars and a handful of change when she left her house. She wrote in her notebook, DEVELOP EMERGENCY SPY FUND.

A movement across the street caught her attention. The surfer was holding the door open for Annie and the curly-haired man, who was toting a Bloomingdale's shopping bag. When all three of them stood on the curb, the curly-haired man set the shopping bag down, reached into his wallet, and handed the surfer a bill. Harriet squinted but couldn't see how big the payoff was. Ten dollars? Twenty? Five hundred? She tossed a tip onto her table and went to the door, being careful to pull up her hood in case Annie should look her way.

The curly-haired man reached into the shopping bag and took out a lavender box, the size of a shoe box but flatter. As he gave it to Annie, the surfer dude suddenly lunged onto East Seventy-second Street, shooting his arm up to flag down a cab. The curly-haired man gave Annie a hasty hug, kissed the top of her head, and shepherded her to the cab. He closed the door after her, leaned down toward the window, and waved. Then he stood at the curb and watched as the cab pulled away.

Emboldened by Annie's departure, Harriet went to the crosswalk. *He* won't recognize me, she figured, and I want a closer look. When the light clicked to WALK, she started across the street and realized that the curly-haired man was heading right toward her. She dipped her head, pretending to look for something in her backpack. As he passed her, she zipped it back up with a sigh of frustration, as if she'd forgotten something important, and turned around, following him down the stairs to the downtown-bound subway.

Harriet hesitated a moment, weighing her parents' directive against riding the subway alone against her intense curiosity. Curiosity won. She went through the turnstile and stood on the platform a few poles away from the man. His coat was cut of a butterscotch-colored cashmere that looked very expensive. His shoes were well shined. But his face didn't look like a gangster's—at least, not the gangsters in movies. He had blue eyes and a long nose with slightly flared nostrils; his unruly curls looked as if they'd been blown by a sea breeze. If she had run into him at the yacht club in Water Mill, Long Island, where her family spent summers, she wouldn't have batted an eye.

The downtown train pulled into the station. The man got on quickly and took a seat next to a couple of black teenage girls with enormous gold earrings. Harriet went in through the same car's far door and positioned herself at a center pole. Only when the train closed its doors and lurched out of the station did it occur to her that the man might be riding to Brooklyn or Queens, maybe even to Kennedy Airport. I'll stay on the case for a couple more stops, she thought, feeling her heart pound, and then I'll decide.

Luckily, he got off at Lexington and Fifty-first Street, a transfer stop Harriet knew well from weekend excursions with Ole Golly. Was he going to the

Museum of Modern Art? It didn't seem likely, but no good spy ever ruled anything out without firsthand proof. She followed him at a discreet distance, pinning her gaze on the sleeve of his butterscotch coat as she stayed behind two German students with oversized backpacks. They arrived at the E train platform.

The man took a seat on an empty bench and reached into his coat pocket, unfolding a long piece of paper and peering at it with a studious frown. That's a *clue*, thought Harriet. I've got to get closer and see what he's reading. She noticed a garbage can next to the bench and riffled through her pockets, searching for something to throw away. There was a wadded-up page that she'd torn from her spy notebook when she'd misspelled a word. Perfect, she thought. All I have to do now is look casual.

She took a deep breath. An easy saunter, she thought, your basic who-cares-about-anything stroll. She balanced the crumpled-up page on the palm of her hand and strolled toward the trash can, slowing down as she passed the bench. The man was squinting at a railroad schedule. Of *course*, thought Harriet, he's on his way to Penn Station. The getaway! She was so thrilled by her spying skills that she nearly forgot to throw out the paper she had in her hand.

Penn Station was vast. Harriet had been to the interstate railway station just once, to see Ole Golly off on the Montrealer, and the thought of navigating that huge maze of tunnels and crossing the vaulting concourse with its crush of commuters and fast-flipping destination signs, without her hand safely clutched in her mother's, was simply too daunting. I'm *twelve*, she thought. I've done all that a spy of my years can be expected to do, maybe more.

Anyway, she reassured herself, I'm supposed to be spying on *Annie*.

An E train clattered into the station. The curly-haired man stuffed the schedule back into his pocket and went to the edge of the platform. The double doors opened and people poured out. Harriet watched the man's back as he stepped on board, still lugging the Bloomingdale's bag. She hated to give up the chase, but as soon as she got to her room, she could write every detail down in her notebook. The thought made her happy. This was a seven-page day, at least. Maybe she'd set a new record.

"Stand clear of the closing doors," a conductor warned. The double doors hissed shut and the train gathered speed. Harriet stood still and watched till its taillights left the station. Then she turned and walked toward the train that would bring her back uptown, and home.

Harriet woke up the next day with her mind full of questions. She looked at the flashlight on her night table, which the night before had flashed its usual nine-thirty semaphore, just as if nothing were different. *Everything's* different, she thought. Her parents had been upset with her lengthy midday disappearance (though not as upset as they would have been if they'd known where she had gone, she consoled herself). Harriet had had enough presence of mind to place a call to Janie, urging her to say, if and when questioned, that they'd been together.

"Where were you really?" Janie had asked.

"That's classified. Urgent spy business."

"Oh." Janie's voice flattened. "That." But she had agreed to hold up the story, so Harriet's only transgression was not having let her parents know in advance where she'd be for three hours. For this, she'd been grounded, and had to spend all day in her house doing homework, no TV, no phone calls. It would be a dull Sunday.

Good time to catch up on my notebooks, she thought. Sometimes Harriet liked to sit down and reread a volume or two to see if she'd failed to report anything of significance. Now she resolved to go all the way back to the first time she'd met Annie, aka Rosarita Sauvage.

Harriet brushed her teeth, dressed, and went down to the kitchen for breakfast. Morning light slanted in from the street-level windows in front and the snow-covered garden in back. She poured cornflakes into her favorite bowl and reached into the fruit bowl for a banana. On the counter beside it, she spotted a letter in Ole Golly's unmistakable back-slanted handwriting, with the dark and light strokes of a chiseled calligraphy pen. It must have arrived in yesterday's mail, she thought. Why didn't anyone *tell* me? She ripped the envelope open and read.

Dear Harriet, Ole Golly had written,

I can no more explain falling in love than I could explain how to breathe. Both are involuntary and both are essential. Poets have pondered the subject for centuries.

Mr. H. L. Mencken edited a superb dictionary of quotations, grouped by topic rather than author. The entries for love run a full sixteen pages. I will leave you with just this one, from Elizabeth Barrett Browning: "Whoever lives true life, will love true love."

As ever,
Catherine Golly Waldenstein

P.S. Promise me that you won't grow up too fast. I want our baby to meet you when you're still my Harriet.

Harriet read the letter three times before she poured milk on her cornflakes. That's really no help, she thought, lifting her spoon to her lips. It certainly doesn't explain Annie's older man.

• • •

Annie met her the next morning in front of her door. "I called you yesterday and your mom wouldn't let you talk. What's up with that, H'spy?"

"I forgot to leave her a note when I went to Janie's on Saturday."

Annie shrugged. "At least she was worried about you. My mother wouldn't have noticed that I was gone. She'd be too busy writing some play."

Harriet's jaw dropped. "Your mother's a playwright?"

"I just said so, didn't I?" Annie snapped.

Harriet looked at her sidelong. Now there were *two* topics she was dying to broach. Which was less likely to set Annie off, she wondered, her mother's career or the older man? Annie stepped up on one of the wrought-iron rails that fenced off the trees on the sidewalk and balanced along its length. "Follow my steps, H'spy. First to fall off is a double-*l* loser," she said, in her best imitation of Marion Hawthorne.

• • •

A thick, swirling snowfall began at the end of the school day. Mr. Grenville was reading a scene from the end of act three of *Romeo and Juliet*, and worked himself into such a frenzy as Juliet's furious father that the teacher next door, Miss Munson, knocked on the wall and yelled, "Quiet!" The whole class dissolved into giggles.

Mr. Grenville looked affronted. He stretched out his arm and read, "Hang thee, young baggage! disobedient wretch!" in more modulated tones. The bell rang and the students tumbled noisily out of their chairs. Mr. Grenville sighed the deep sigh of the misunderstood.

The sidewalk was white with an inch of new snowfall. Annie and Harriet tried out different gaits, leaving strange-looking footprints by dragging one foot in a zigzagging line or walking on tiptoe. At one point they walked back to back with their arms linked, leaving twin rows of chevrons, like this:

> <

> <

> <

"Let's go to the tree stand and see what Balsam and Douglas Fir do when it snows," Annie said.

"They get snowy," said Harriet.

Annie poked her. "You know what I mean. Do they put up tarps? Take in the trees? We haven't been there all weekend."

"We couldn't," said Harriet, sensing an opening. "You had to go to that Hanukkah thing with your aunt and uncle." Her tone was distinctly pointed.

"And *you* went to Janie's," said Annie.

Is she calling my bluff? wondered Harriet. She tried a different approach. "Are you buying a Hanukkah gift for your older man?"

Annie looked appalled. "I would never do anything so cheap and obvious. That would be tacky."

She swept off down the street. Harriet followed. She didn't like the idea of spying on Balsam and Douglas so soon after Balsam had caught them, but she wasn't about to let Annie get away without answering some questions. As they crossed the street toward the Koreans', she noticed a column of smoke rising out of a trash can. Balsam threw in some cut branches, and Douglas upended a large metal trash can. Flames leaped through the can's perforations.

Annie grabbed Harriet's arm. "Look!" she whispered. "They're burning the evidence!"

"What evidence?"

"Aha," Annie said. "That's the mystery."

"I think they're burning the wood chips and paper bags."

"Shows what you know. The Dumbwit's a document forger. You think he sits on that stool reading his book all day long, but he's grinding out phony savings bonds right in the back of that truck. Myong-Hee's the connection. They've opened an offshore account in the Bahamas."

Harriet rolled her eyes. "Could we please stick to the facts?"

"Facts"—Annie spit out the word—"are a bore."

Not in my world, thought Harriet. I'm going to find out the facts about *you.*

• • •

"Did you notice the Dumbwit's jeans?" Annie said as they walked to the Feigenbaums'. "The knees are so ripped you can see the ripped long johns. I tell you, H'spy, these are desperate men. They're losing the farm and the only way out is a life of crime. Balsam is going to run off to Las Vegas to marry Myong-Hee and Douglas will be so upset that he'll go on a killing spree. We'll read about it in the *New York Post*. 'Christmas Tree Massacre.' "

"Have you seen a lot of massacres?" Harriet asked shrewdly.

"Dozens," said Annie.

She's not going to give me a straight answer, ever, thought Harriet. Trying to conjure up Mr. Grenville's dramatic skills, she let out a big phony shiver. "My feet are like ice. Let's go inside and make cocoa."

"Food's better at your place."

She's trying to steer me away, thought Harriet, more determined than ever to spy on the Feigenbaums. She pulled a face. "I was stuck in my stupid apartment all yesterday. I need a change of scenery."

"If you must," said Annie, and led her inside. The Feigenbaums' receptionist looked up from her desk and smiled at them. Harriet's eyes swept the waiting room as they walked past to the private part of the house. The tall man rubbing his knees was a Morris, for sure; the too-thin woman with bulging eyes could go either way. Probably a Barbara, Harriet thought, with a hormone disorder, or trying some test-tubey way to get pregnant.

Or, she thought, both well-disguised Mafiosi. After the men in the seafood restaurant, anything was possible. She followed Annie down the back stairs.

Annie made them both cocoa, which, Harriet noticed, had sugar and marshmallows this time around. There were even some packages of cookies. Annie's exerting her influence over the Feigenbaums, Harriet thought. Might be significant.

Both of the patients were gone by the time the girls went upstairs to Annie's room. It was a guest bedroom, layered with old Oriental rugs and painted a dim shade of russet, with still lifes and zoological etchings in frames on the walls. No visible effort had been made to redecorate it for a twelve-year-old girl, but Harriet's sharp eyes immediately landed on two items she hadn't seen before. The first was a well-worn sock monkey tucked next to the pillow. The second, which made her pulse race, was the lavender box the curly-haired man had thrust into Annie's hands as she'd gotten into the cab on Saturday. It's a love gift, thought Harriet. I *have* to find out what's inside.

It seemed like a very long time until Annie got up to go the bathroom. As soon as she heard the door click, Harriet sprang to her feet and took off the top of the box, covering her fingers with her sleeve so as not to leave fingerprints. Inside was a handwritten note and a long, narrow ticket envelope. She scanned the note feverishly. It read *Here's Mr. Monkey. He missed you. So do I. xx, P.*

Harriet's heart took a lurch at that *xx, P.* She had an initial! And everyone knew that *x*'s meant kisses. Someone whose name started with P had sent Annie kisses—and, of all inexplicable things, a childish sock monkey that didn't, on closer inspection, appear to be all that clean. Whoever P. was, his idea of what one should give to a sophisticated twelve-year-old girl was wildly off base.

She lifted the note in one sleeve-covered hand and picked up the envelope in the other. It wasn't that easy to open it without the full use of her fingers, and before she was able to wiggle the ticket out so she could see it, the toilet flushed down the hall. Harriet scrambled to put the note and envelope back and replace the lid. She was still standing up when she heard Annie's footsteps outside the door, so she looked out the window to cover.

"It's snowing a *lot*," she said. "Maybe they'll cancel school."

"I used to love snow days in Boston," said Annie, her voice sounding mournful for just a split second before she bounced back with "I bet they get plenty of snow days up north in New Hampshire. Not that that matters to dropouts."

• • •

The week flew past. Each day, the Feigenbaums twisted another bulb into the electric menorah in their front window. The girls at the Gregory School were buzzing with Christmas vacation plans, and one teacher after another plastered the walls with seasonal cutouts. Harriet wondered if there was some kind of holiday vest rule: it seemed that every teacher and even the school nurse, Mrs. Kelder, came in wearing a vest embroidered with holly or candy canes.

Harriet had decided to buy a calligraphy pen like Ole Golly's and make her parents a limited-edition collection of her favorite poems. She asked Annie if she'd like to make a Saturday afternoon pilgrimage to Jasmine's Art Supply, but Annie demurred, saying she already had plans.

I bet you do, Harriet thought. Plans with P. She resolved to keep her eyes glued to the Feigenbaums' house on Saturday. Right after school on Friday, she went to the bank with her mother and made a withdrawal, "for certain upcoming expenses." As expected, Harriet's mother smiled at her fondly and took the bait, saying, "As long as you know that the most special presents are always the ones you make yourself." It wasn't entirely a lie, Harriet reassured herself; although most of the money would go directly to her new Emergency Spy Fund, she did plan to buy the calligraphy pen for making her parents' gift.

It took her a full hour to pick out just the right pen and paper at Jasmine's Friday afternoon. There were all sorts of creamy linen and textured rice papers, and deckle-edged cardstocks in every hue. Finally she selected five sheets of a handcrafted paper with small flecks of marigold petals. While the clerk rolled them into a tube, Harriet's eye roamed a shelf of bound sketchbooks and landed on one with a marbled blue cover. That's gorgeous, she thought. It'd make a great journal. Not a spy notebook, but something more elegant: notes from a grand tour of Europe, for instance. She picked it up, checking the price. Underneath was a second book, just like the first, except that the marbled design was in shades of deep red. I bet Annie would like that for Hanukkah, Harriet thought. Or for Christmas. Or both.

"Will that be all?" asked the clerk, a slim Japanese girl with sculptural earrings.

Harriet paused. She would have loved to buy both of the books, but they cost too much. "And this," she said, handing the clerk the red sketchbook.

That evening, she cut the marigold papers and sewed them together, using the bookbinder's stitch she'd learned from her art teacher, Mrs. Nussbaum. Now all she needed to do was select the poems. Which would give her a perfect excuse to spend Saturday in the library, waiting for Annie to leave her apartment. This time she had a prearranged cover: she'd told her parents she would be spending a couple of hours with Sport in the park.

By midafternoon she had three times as many poems as she could fit into the book she had made. She was flipping through a volume of poems by Edgar Allan Poe with woodcut illustrations, kind of creepy for Christmas but hard to put down, when she saw Annie leave through the side alley gate. She was wearing her red beret and clutching something Harriet recognized as the ticket envelope she'd seen in the lavender box.

Harriet jumped to her feet, grabbed her backpack and parka, and yelled up to her parents, "I'm going to Sport's now, okay?" She rushed out before they could answer.

Harriet tailed Annie's footprints west in the new-dusted snow, even though she was certain where Annie was heading. Sure enough, she walked straight to the Papaya King stand. This time the surfer guy with the blond beard met her right at the door, flashing a crooked grin that made Harriet flush unexpectedly. He's kind of cute, she was startled to find herself thinking; I would have picked *him* over P. There was no time to dwell on this unexpected sensation—she had to move quickly before Annie saw her. She bent to the pavement, pretending to tie her shoe, and was rather embarrassed to realize, slightly too late, that her boots had no laces. *That's* pretty lame, thought Harriet, with her ears flaming. I hope he's not paying attention.

She stole a glance up from the sidewalk as the surfer waved down a cab with long-armed grace. Harriet's heart raced when she realized that he wore fingerless gloves, just like hers. Whoever he is, he has *great* luck with cabs, she thought as Annie slid into the back and he followed her, shutting the door.

Harriet's heart sank. Tailing a bus on foot had been almost impossible; she could never keep up with a Manhattan cabbie. She looked at the oncoming block of traffic and was astonished to see, amid dozens of occupied cabs, one that was just clicking its roof light back on after letting a passenger out at the corner. Her hand shot up like a basketball player's, and she waved her fingerless glove as the stoplight turned from yellow to red. Come on, she prayed silently. Do it.

The cab driver floored the gas pedal and ran the red light, squealing up to the curb. Harriet leaped into the backseat and shouted the order she'd longed to give for her whole spy career: "Follow that cab!"

CHAPTER 8

The two taxicabs hurtled downtown. Harriet's driver was a jovial man with a pointy black beard and a lilting West African accent; his license tag named him as Quiah Sissoko. He was listening to zouk on the radio, and the air in the cab smelled improbably of strawberry perfume, probably from one of the charms that hung from his rearview mirror. "Where they going?" he asked Harriet.

"Downtown," she said hastily, then added, in case that sounded incomplete, "My sister forgot something I need to give her."

"Ah," said the driver. "You want me to honk at the next light?"

"*No!*" she practically shouted, and then added limply, "She might be embarrassed."

The cabdriver shrugged. "It's your dollar."

They drove down Fifth Avenue, past Central Park and the Plaza Hotel. There were glittery garlands and Christmas-themed shop windows everywhere. Finally Annie's cab pulled over, just outside the entrance to Rockefeller Center. Harriet's cab pulled over behind it. "You go see the big tree?" asked the driver, beaming at her. "It's fantastic. I took my three kids on the first night they lit it."

Harriet handed him money and lunged for the door.

"Your change!" he called.

"Keep it," she said, jumping onto the curb. "Merry Christmas!" Annie and her escort were moving away from her fast, and Harriet was sure she'd lose sight of them in the huge crowd of tourists. She fastened her sights on the man's blond head—because he was taller, she told herself; Annie's beret could get lost in a crush of big shoulders.

They were passing between two tall buildings, on a double path split by a long row of topiary reindeer. Snatches of carols drifted out from boutiques on both sides, but as they drew close to the plaza where the gigantic Christmas tree stood, the amplified sound from the skating rink drowned out the rest of the music. Annie stopped in her tracks to gape up at the twinkling enormity of the great tree, and Harriet realized that this was Annie Smith's first New York City Christmas.

Someone waved from the corner rail of the skating rink. Harriet recognized him at once as the cashmere-clad man with the curly hair, the older man Annie had met in the restaurant. It's P., she thought. Twice in two weeks. She squinted at Annie to see if she showed any telltale shifts in behavior, but Annie's expression was hard to read. She walked toward the skating rink, and the blond guy went with her, laying a casual hand on her shoulder.

He was wearing the same Guatemalan wool jacket he'd had on the first time Harriet had seen him. It suited him. But it was that fingerless glove resting on her friend's shoulder that stirred up a feeling that made her feel stupid, embarrassed, and happy at once. It could *not* be a crush, she told herself sternly. Not on a spy mission.

She watched as the three of them met at the edge of the rink. This time the older man hugged Annie first, then turned to her escort, shaking his hand and clapping him on the back before handing over a folded bill.

The blond guy gave Annie a half bow and waved

goodbye, turning to amble back toward Fifth Avenue. Harriet froze in her tracks. He was heading right toward her. If she turned away to hide her face and protect her anonymity, she would certainly lose sight of Annie and P. He doesn't know me from Adam, she thought. I'll just brazen it out and walk past him like any other tourist who's come here to look at the tree. She took several steps forward as he approached and realized that he was looking right at her. Worse, he was gesturing, making eye contact.

"Nice gloves." He grinned, flashing a bare-fingered peace sign.

"Thanks," croaked Harriet, blushing beet red.

• • •

The crowd was so dense by the tree and the skating rink that it was hard to maneuver at all, much less keep a discreet eye on Annie and P. Once or twice Harriet thought she had lost them for sure, but she always managed to spot Annie's red beret between elbows and backs. When they emerged onto Sixth Avenue, there was no question where they were headed: Radio City Music Hall. Of course, thought Harriet as Annie took her ticket envelope out of her pocket. The Christmas show!

Uniformed ushers tore tickets briskly in front of each door. P. put his arm around Annie's shoulders and led her in, past a maroon velvet rope. There was no way to follow them into the lobby without a ticket. Harriet stood underneath the marquee, looking at the sleek art deco doors, and tried to decide what to do with herself. Should she just head back home? Watch the skaters or go Christmas shopping? Or find a good place for a stakeout and follow them after the show?

This last option promised the most satisfaction. Harriet asked one of the ushers how long the first act would run and found out she had more than an hour to wait. She decided to circle around to the back of the building and look for a place where she could sit down with her notebook until intermission.

The bray of a donkey surprised her; it wasn't a sound you expected to hear in midtown Manhattan. Harriet turned quickly, trying to pinpoint the source, and spotted a couple of grumpy-looking stagehands unloading a truck full of livestock. The donkey came down the ramp first, led by a teenage girl in a 4-H sweatshirt. Next came a camel that hissed and spit, balking on top of the ramp. It took three or four handlers to coax it out of the truck and down to the pavement. The stagehands shook their heads, cursing. The younger one glared at his crew-cut boss and said, "This is the last time I work on a living Nativity."

"If that camel kicks a Rockette, it's the last time you're gonna work, period," growled the boss, pushing him through the stage door.

Harriet waited. She heard sounds of bleating from inside the truck, but nobody else came out. Maybe all the 4-H volunteers were already in the theater. She looked up the ramp, wondering how many sheep were making that racket, when she was struck by an outrageous idea. "I couldn't," she said out loud, and answered herself, "Annie would."

She looked at the stage door again. It was propped open a crack with a stage weight so that it wouldn't lock while they led in the animals. Harriet's heart seemed to thump in her throat as she crept up to it, swiveling her head to make sure no one saw her, and slipped inside.

The backstage was as bare as the lobby was glitzy. There was a warren of dimly lit halls and a metal staircase that led down to the dressing room. Harriet spotted a couple of telltale straws of hay on the floor and walked that way, passing a group of dancers in candy cane outfits. Look sure of yourself, she thought, lifting her chin as though she had every right in the world to be strolling around in the wings of the most famous stage in America.

There it was, right up ahead. Harriet gaped at the

ceiling, which seemed to be hundreds of feet overhead, crisscrossed by fly pipes and a schooner's worth of rigging and ropes. The back wall was brick, with antique radiators in vertical rows. The huge velvet curtain was backed with plain canvas, stenciled FIRE BARRIER. Freestanding pieces of scenery stood in the wings at odd angles: a candy cane archway, a *Nutcracker* ballroom, a set of chrome stairs. Harriet watched as a couple of technicians with headsets crossed the vast stage. One peered up at the light bridge, while a second reset the triangular wooden braces behind a big backdrop.

"Excuse me." A stern voice cut across the air. Harriet turned and found herself facing a tiny woman, barely her height, dressed from top to toe in black with a little red star on her cap. She wore a headset and carried a stage manager's clipboard. "You can't be backstage."

Harriet stammered and flushed. She would have to think fast. "My—my cousin," she croaked, "she's a Rockette. She said I could watch from the wings."

"Where's your stage pass?"

"My bus came in late from New Jersey," said Harriet. "I was afraid I would miss the beginning. I didn't even have time to go down to her dressing room and hang up my parka or anything." Her voice had begun to take on a New Jerseyesque twang. This is actually fun, she thought. No wonder Annie makes up different personalities.

The stage manager's eyes were still narrowed, as if she was not quite convinced. Harriet met her eye, trying to look as if she might weep if this didn't work out. "I came in from Hackensack special," she pleaded. "How long till it starts?"

"We're at five," the stage manager said. "Five minutes to places."

"You want me to go find my cousin and get the backstage pass?" said Harriet, praying that the answer was no. The stage manager looked her right in the eye.

"What's your cousin's name?" she said.

"Emma," said Harriet, thinking of one of the girls in the dance class she'd taken with Janie the previous fall. The stage manager frowned, so she blurted, "Her stage name is Lily." She held her breath, hoping there was a Rockette by that name. Apparently so; the stage manager softened her gaze and nodded. "I'll show you the best place to sit."

• • •

Harriet perched on a stool just behind the prop table, scribbling down details in her green notebook. She noticed that each item was labeled, with its spot on the table outlined in masking tape, so the prop master could see at a glance whether every prop was in place. Systems like this appealed to Harriet. She resolved to draw outlines of every item she had in her backpack when she got home. She unzipped it, took out a pair of bird-watching binoculars that her father had given her, and scanned the triangular wedge of the audience visible to her from this angle, searching for Annie and P. If I get to spy on them from *here*, she thought, from the backstage of the Radio City Music Hall Christmas Show, it'll be one for the record books.

She worked her way up and down every row but recognized no one. They must have seats on the opposite side of the audience, Harriet thought, disappointed. She was about to replace the binoculars when she noticed a man and a girl sidling past a row of people who stood back for them, perching on top of their seats.

Harriet trained her binoculars right on that row. Sure enough, it was Annie and P., who was clutching a large box of Milk Duds. They reached their seats just as the house lights dimmed. Harriet stared at their faces. Neither of them had the enraptured expression secret lovers in movies always had when they went on a rendezvous; Annie, in fact, looked as if she might burst into tears any minute.

There were only four days left until winter break, and the halls of the Gregory School were ringing with talk about Christmas vacations. Everyone seemed to be going someplace where she could get tan: the Caribbean, a ski resort, Greece. Beth Ellen Hansen was taking a cruise.

"Where are *you* going, Cassandra?" said Marion Hawthorne, who'd just told the group near her locker that her parents had rented a bungalow on Guadeloupe.

"The family villa in Sicily," Annie replied. "If my uncles are done with their squabble, that is. Otherwise I'll just be stuck in Las Vegas."

Marion and Rachel exchanged wary glances and

nodded. “Have fun,” Rachel said, scuttling down the hall so fast she looked like an insect.

• • •

“Are you really going away during break?” Harriet asked as she walked Annie home.

“Where would I go?” Annie’s voice was forlorn. “I’m not supposed to go back to Boston till everything’s settled, and my aunt and uncle are working straight through the vacation. My uncle says his patients all get depressed at the holidays, and my aunt’s patients just keep on having babies. Anyway, they don’t celebrate Christmas. Not even a tree.” She cast a yearning look over at Balsam and Douglas’s tree stand. Harriet had the urge to reach out and take her friend’s arm, but she stopped herself, remembering how Annie had bristled the last time she’d tried that. She doesn’t want anyone pitying her, thought Harriet.

“That’s a nice scarf,” she said. “Is it new?”

“Thanks.” Annie smiled, but her voice sounded scratchy. “My mom sent it to me for Hanukkah.” She wrapped the scarf tighter around her throat.

• • •

When Harriet got home, she was delighted to find a square envelope with her name on it next to the usual stack of bills in the foyer. The stamp was Canadian. She took the stairs two at a time on the way to the third floor and brought the card into Ole Golly's old bedroom to read it. The front showed a woman in white in her garden with two little girls. Her expression was tender. Harriet opened the card.

Harriet M., it read. Harriet smiled, remembering how Ole Golly had called her that when she was little.

I've been pondering the question you posed in your last letter. You asked about love, and I answered, as most people probably would, with regard to romantic love. But as I feel my baby beginning to stir and kick, I am newly aware of the many ways in which human beings can love. Parents love. Friends love. Sometimes even spies love. The world is a rich and remarkable place. But it is not, repeat, not sentimental.

As ever,
Catherine Golly Waldenstein

P.S. Isn't this painting miraculous? You can practically smell the wisteria.

• • •

Cook had made lamb chops, juicy and red in the small curve of bone. Harriet was glad when her father picked up a rib, gnawing the last of the meat with his teeth. Her mother was conscious of good table manners, and Harriet, who had eaten her dinners downstairs in the kitchen with Ole Golly for years, was still wary of what might be deemed impolite. She picked up a rib with her fingers and followed her father's example.

"You look like Neanderthals," her mother said.

"Oh, for God's sake, woman, let us be carnivores," Harriet's father said, winking at Harriet. "We're not at a White House banquet."

"Nor at a clambake on Long Island Sound."

Harriet set down her bone, dabbing her fingers discreetly with a napkin before she picked up the right fork. "Mom?" she ventured.

"Yes, dear?"

"Are we going to go to Long Island for Christmas?"

"Of course we are, Harriet. I wouldn't miss it," her father said.

"Your father insists that the Upper East Side isn't windy and cold enough," Harriet's mother said, smiling. "It's not a real Christmas unless you get chilled to the bone every time you go out."

"Beaches are best at off-season," her father said, chomping a lamb chop.

"I agree," said her mother. "Bermuda is lovely in August."

"Could I invite Annie?" asked Harriet. Both parents looked at her. "She's going to be all by herself over Christmas. Her uncle and aunt are just going to work."

"I think that would be lovely," said Harriet's mother. "It'd be nice for you to have someone your age there, and that poor girl has had such a difficult autumn. Let me speak to the Feigenbaums. Harry?"

"If it makes Harriet happy, it's all right by me," said her father, helping himself to some more mashed potatoes and sloshing the pile with a huge wave of gravy.

"Pour with the spout, not the side," said her mother, smiling indulgently. "Honestly, Harry, you're hopeless."

• • •

Barbara Feigenbaum said that a couple of days near the ocean would "do the girl good," and Annie seemed vastly relieved to get out of the city. I wonder how P. feels about her leaving town, Harriet thought as she glanced across the backseat at her friend, but there was no way she could ask.

There wasn't much snow on Montauk Highway. Here and there on the roadside the sea winds had carved off big snowdrifts like dunes. Harriet gazed out the window, remembering how she and Beth Ellen Hansen had raced down this road on their bicycles just a few months before, the sun at their backs and the wind in their hair.

Mrs. Welsch turned around in the passenger seat. "Have you ever been out to Long Island before, Annie?"

"No," Annie said. "But it looks like Cape Cod."

"We spent our honeymoon on the Cape, didn't we, Harry? The darling old windmill in Truro. Those *dunes*. And the breakers! I'll never forget it."

Annie listened politely as Harriet's mother rattled on about chowder and Portuguese fisherman's soup with chorizo and kale.

My mother means well, thought Harriet, watching her friend, but she doesn't know when a person prefers to be left alone.

• • •

The beach house was drafty, so Mrs. Welsch drove the girls to the supermarket while Mr. Welsch lit a fire in the grate. They had already unpacked a big cooler of groceries that they had brought from New York, because one couldn't count on finding fresh produce outside the city at this time of year. Cook had baked a buffet's worth of pies and packed several dinners in lidded casseroles, but Mrs. Welsch had insisted on roasting the holiday turkey herself. "I'm not helpless," she said with a sniff. Cook's nod was, at best, noncommital.

Still, there were staples to buy. "Let's get a ton of food," Harriet said. "Let's buy *everything*!"

Her mother smiled. "That salt air goes right to your appetite. What do you eat for breakfast?" she asked, turning to Annie, who shrugged.

"My aunt mostly serves Cream of Wheat," she said. "Or yogurt."

"But what do you *like*?"

Annie looked first at Harriet, then at her mother. "French toast and bacon," she said. "With hash brown potatoes."

"Then that's what we'll have," said Mrs. Welsch. Good for you, Mom, thought Harriet.

• • •

The girls spent the afternoon decorating the beach house for Christmas. They folded white paper into tight squares and cut on the folds to make snowflakes. They dug out an old set of tempera paints that weren't too dried up and decorated a bucket of seashells and pine cones with glitter and paint, and used bent paper clips to make ornament hangers.

They popped popcorn and strung it with cranberries, muttering whenever the needle and thread broke the kernels in half. All they needed now was the tree. "We should have bought one at Balsam's," said Harriet.

"Where's that?" said her mother.

"The stand on the corner of East Eighty-eighth," said Annie. "Next to the Koreans'."

"No need to pay clip-joint markups," said Harriet's father. "We're out in the country." He went to his tool bench and picked out an orange-handled crosscut saw.

"Who wants to go on an expedition?" he said. Annie and Harriet raised their hands, as if they were at school. "You're hired," he said, grinning.

"Wrap up," urged Mrs. Welsch. "The wind off the bay's like a knife."

• • •

Annie and Mrs. Welsch washed and dried the dinner dishes while Harriet held the tree upright and Mr. Welsch got on his knees to tighten the screws of the heavy green tree stand. "Is it straight?" he asked. "Tell me it's straight."

Harriet took a few steps back, and the tree lurched in the other direction. "Not anymore."

Mr. Welsch banged the tree back into place. "We can put men on the moon," he mumbled, retightening screws, "but try to design a Christmas tree stand that works . . ."

"You say that every year, Daddy."

"I'd be the richest man in America."

"You say that, too."

Mrs. Welsch came back into the room, casting a critical eye at the tree. "It's leaning a little."

Her husband growled. "Which direction?"

Annie appeared in the doorway behind Mrs. Welsch. They said, "That way," in unison, leaning their hands in two different directions.

"Well, that's good enough for me." Mr. Welsch got to his feet, dusting off his knees. "Better get out that vacuum before all these needles get ground into the carpet. And test out those twinkle lights. They've been in the attic all year."

"Oh, Harry," said Mrs. Welsch, sliding her arms around his waist. "It's a beautiful tree. The best ever."

"It is pretty nice," he admitted, leaning his cheek on the top of her head as he surveyed the Christmas tree, framed by the wide plate-glass window that looked out on the ice-frosted beach.

"You know what we didn't buy? Mistletoe."

"Mistletoe," said Mr. Welsch, kissing her, "would be redundant."

Harriet looked over at Annie, whose arms had been folded across her chest ever since Mr. and Mrs. Welsch had embraced. She turned and walked quickly out of the room.

Mrs. Welsch swiveled her head. "Oh dear," she said softly. "Maybe I'd better—"

"Mom." Harriet's voice was clipped. "Leave her alone, okay?"

• • •

Harriet set her toothbrush back in the glass and looked in the mirror at Annie. "It feels strange to get ready for bed without doing semaphore," she offered.

"I guess," Annie said. They walked into the bedroom, and Harriet got in her bed. The sheets were so cold that she shivered and drew the quilt up to her chin. They'll warm up soon, she thought. Annie climbed into the trundle bed.

"The last person to sleep in that bed was Beth Ellen."

"Beth Ellen *Hansen*? Beth Ellen the mouse?"

"She's not such a mouse as you think," said Harriet, and told Annie how, during the summer, she and Beth Ellen had been spies together, trying to figure out who had been leaving hand-lettered quotations, usually from the Bible and usually very unflattering, for people in every corner of Water Mill.

"And guess who was doing it?" Harriet said.

"How would *I* know?" said Annie sharply. "I don't know anyone here."

"You know this one," said Harriet. "Beth Ellen was doing it."

"Really?"

Harriet nodded. "She tried to throw me off the track by pretending to join in the search, but I bagged her." She examined Annie's face in the moonlight.

Annie looked thoughtful. "Was Beth Ellen mad when you caught her?"

Harriet shook her head. "I think she was actually kind of relieved," she said, watching closely for Annie's reaction. "Sometimes it's hard to keep secrets."

"Sometimes," said Annie, "you don't have a choice." She rolled over and stared at the wall.

Another dead end, thought Harriet. Oh well. I tried. She looked up at the ceiling, where she could still see the ghosts of the glow-in-the-dark stars she'd stuck up there when she was in second grade. The sound of the breakers was rhythmic, soothing. It was always so easy to fall asleep next to the ocean.

"Sweet dreams," she said. Annie didn't respond.

Harriet looked at the trundle and saw that her shoulders were shaking beneath the quilt. "Annie?"

"You're so lucky, H'spy." Annie sniffed. "You still have parents."

• • •

Christmas morning was blustery. The water was gunmetal gray with white combers, and wind swirled the traces of snow on the deck. There were intricate patterns of frost on the sliding glass doors.

Mr. Welsch made the girls bacon, hash browns, and French toast with whipped cream and red and green sprinkles. They all ate in bathrobes and slippers. It seemed to take Mrs. Welsch hours to wash all the dishes so they could sit down at the foot of the tree and start opening presents. Harriet watched Annie closely, wondering if she was still feeling left out and sad. If she was, she was hiding it well.

Finally Harriet's mother sat down on the couch. "Who's going to be the elf?" asked her father.

"Let's be our own elves," said Harriet, sounding a bit irritated. "We're not six years old. We can find our own presents."

"An elven rebellion," said Mr. Welsch, raising his eyebrows. "All right. Every elf for himself." They plunged into the pile.

There were too many presents, as usual, some that made people happy and some that produced frozen smiles. Mr. Welsch was especially irked by a shirt his wife had picked out. "How long have you known me? I don't wear striped shirts. I wear white shirts and blue shirts; on weekends I sometimes wear plaid shirts. I've never liked stripes."

"Well, I just thought a change would be nice."

"If I craved a change, I would not start with stripes."

"There's no need to snipe at me, Harry. I'll take it back."

Harriet noticed that Annie had turned her head. She seemed to be staring at something outside on the deck, but Harriet had the impression that her thoughts were elsewhere, perhaps with her own parents. Harriet picked up a gift wrapped in three different colors of tissue. "For you," she said.

Annie opened it, snaking the long ribbon down to the floor and unfurling the layers of tissue. She stared at the red marble sketchbook in silence.

"What's the matter?" asked Harriet.

Annie picked up a package wrapped in paper with blue and gold six-pointed stars. "For you," she said. "Open it up, H'spy."

Harriet peeled off the paper. Inside was a blue

marbled sketchbook, exactly like Annie's. She looked up at Annie. "Did you get this from—"

"Jasmine's," said Annie. They looked at each other and burst out laughing. Ole Golly was right, thought Harriet, grinning so wide that it practically hurt. There are all kinds of love in this world.

Two days after Christmas, they took down the crooked tree, locked up the house, and drove back to Manhattan. Annie went back to the Feigenbaums', where, she reported, her uncle was on some new diet. That evening, one of Barbara's patients went into labor with premature twins, and she disappeared into the hospital. Annie called Harriet up the next morning. "I'm going out of my skull over here. It's just me, Uncle Morris, and the loon parade. Let's go sled in the park or something."

"Sledding sounds great," said Harriet. Her cousins Jeffrey and Marc had sent her a shovel-shaped French plastic sled they called a butt-slider, and she was dying to try it.

"Do you have two sleds? Mine's in Boston."

"I have three," said Harriet. "A toboggan, a flying saucer, and this French butt-slider. Want to ask Sport?"

"I'd prefer not to," said Annie. "Meet me on the corner in ten."

Harriet put on a ski turtleneck and her Norwegian sweater, then wrapped herself up in a down vest, a long scarf, and snow pants. She found waterproof mitts to go over her fingerless gloves. By the time she left the apartment, waddling in all those layers, she was overheated and sweating.

Annie stood on the corner, as if they were walking to school. She took the toboggan from Harriet and they trudged uptown toward the Koreans'. When they got to the corner, they stopped in their tracks.

The vacant lot was . . . vacant. Not a trace of the Christmas tree stand remained. If not for the ruts where the truck had been parked, no one would have known they had been there at all. Annie stared, speechless.

"They're *gone*," said Harriet, shocked into saying the obvious. "I guess they went back to New Hampshire. I wonder if Balsam ever told Myong-Hee he loved her."

Annie burst into tears. "It's too late."

Harriet stared. "What's the matter with *you?*" she demanded, and Annie let out a heart-wrenching wail.

"I'll never see Douglas again," she sobbed.

"Douglas?" said Harriet. She was incredulous. "Douglas the Dumbwit?"

Annie nodded, sniffling defiantly. "I *told* you I was in love with an older man."

"I don't get it."

"He's not dumb at *all*. I just said that to . . . I don't know why. I just said it."

Harriet shook her head. "That's not what I meant. If Douglas Fir was your older man, who is that guy who took you out to lunch? And to Radio City?"

Annie turned slowly. The color had drained from her face, and her mouth was an angry straight line. "You've been following me. What are you, some kind of double agent?"

"What do you mean?" asked Harriet, stung. Everyone knew double agents were traitors who turned on the people who trusted them most.

"You were spying on *me?*"

Harriet shrugged. "Well, of course. I'm a spy."

"Oh," Annie said. "I thought you were a friend." And she stormed away.

• • •

No semaphore signals were flashed for the rest of vacation. Harriet called several times, and once Annie answered. As soon as she heard who it was, her voice went cold. "Nobody here by that name," she said frostily. "This is Rosarita Sauvage."

She'll stop being mad when we go back to school, thought Harriet. But she waited in vain at the corner on their first day back: Annie had left her house early so she wouldn't have to run into her former best friend. When they stood at their side-by-side lockers, Annie turned her back, slamming the door when Harriet called her by name. This stinks, thought Harriet, watching her clomp down the hall.

The day was an agony. Nobody else spoke to Harriet either. Janie was lost to her new Christmas headphones, on which she could play Jason Orlando tapes in the hall between classes. In the locker room, the popularity clones were all showing off ski tans and photos of beach resorts, chattering like a pack of tropical birds. Marion Hawthorne turned toward Annie. "How was *your* Christmas, Cassandra?"

"It was fine," Annie said, adding darkly, "except for the traitor."

• • •

Harriet pulled on her pajamas, the same pair she'd worn in Water Mill. It felt like a lifetime ago that she'd been so carefree and happy, had sat on the rug cutting snowflakes with Annie, had slept side by side in the trundle bed, gazing at the faded stars on the ceiling. She felt utterly and completely alone. Not even her notebooks distracted her. She stared at a blank page for what felt like hours, but all she could manage to write was

ANNIE WON'T SPEAK TO ME. WHY IS SHE ACTING SO SHOCKED? SHE KNOWS PERFECTLY WELL I TAKE NOTES. I'M A SPY AND A WRITER. WHAT ELSE AM I SUPPOSED TO DO??

What else indeed, she thought, closing the cover. She threw the green notebook back into her trunk, next to the marbled blue sketchbook, and took out the stationery Ole Golly had given her.

Dear Ole Golly, she wrote,

I am having a personal problem. You told me that I should write everything down, and I have. But all is not well. Remember my friend Rosarita, who lived with the Feigenbaums? Her real name is Annie, and she is furious with me. I don't think she'll ever forgive me. I know you're concerned with your upcoming baby and hope all is well in that area

She looked at *area*, frowning, and crossed the word out.

that department, but I need your help.

Harriet stopped writing. How can she help me? she thought. She's in Canada. And no grown-up could possibly understand how this feels.

• • •

Annie didn't bend. She avoided Harriet in the halls and kept to herself in class. She wore clothes that were almost like costumes: a man's derby hat, thrift-store jewelry, unmatched striped socks. Marion and her sidekicks, Carrie and Rachel, made jeering comments whenever they passed in the hall, and when Annie ignored them, pronounced in a stage whisper meant to be overheard, "She is *so* weird."

One day after school, Harriet came upstairs from her cake and milk and heard her mother talking to some other woman behind the closed door of the library. It must be one of her idiot friends from the bridge club, thought Harriet, speeding up so she wouldn't be forced to make conversation. With one foot on the staircase, she stopped short when she recognized the second voice as Barbara Feigenbaum's.

"I don't know what to do with that girl. She comes home from school, slams her door, and goes on these crying jags. Hours she spends crying. If I try to go in and comfort her, she has a tantrum. Morris says it's a needed catharsis, that she trusts us enough to display her repressed emotions, but I just have a feeling that something has changed."

"In what way?" Harriet heard the tinkling stir of a teaspoon on china. They were both drinking tea, she surmised, so this might be a long conversation. She edged toward the door, being careful to stay to one side so that they wouldn't see her feet under its bottom edge.

"Boy trouble, maybe." Harriet held back a snort. Why did everyone think that whatever was wrong with a girl was because of a boy?

Barbara Feigenbaum went on. "She just doesn't seem like herself. I wondered if Harriet had mentioned anything. Maybe something at school?"

"I wish I could help you, but Harriet isn't much of a talker. She takes everything in, but she's very still-waters-run-deep." Am I? thought Harriet, wondering at this description. I thought I was rather loud.

Her mother continued. "She's always up there in her room, writing things down in those notebooks of hers. I'm lucky if I get two words from her."

This was a fascinating perspective to get on herself. Could it even be true? I *don't* really talk to my mother that much, thought Harriet. What would we talk about? Shopping? Bridge? Recipes? She spends all her time doing things that don't interest me. But I never knew she minded.

Barbara Feigenbaum let out a sigh. "It's the age. So much going on in those little heads."

"If you like, I'll ask Harriet point-blank. She doesn't seem to be spending as much time with Annie as usual. Maybe they're spatting."

Spatting? thought Harriet. What trunk did she drag that one out of?

Barbara sighed again. "I'm at my wit's end, I'm telling you. My heart breaks for that child, what she's been through with all this upheaval. It's dragged on for months. My poor sister's a wreck. I can't wait till this nightmare is over."

Harriet's ears perked up. Now they were getting somewhere. *What* nightmare? she thought. I want details. Maybe I'll even find out about P.

"I'm sure," Mrs. Welsch sounded sympathetic. "It's been so hard on all of you."

"Hardest on Annie," said Barbara Feigenbaum. She loves her niece, Harriet realized. The Feigenbaums seemed so entirely clueless, off in their own child-free world, that it had never occurred to her that they really cared about Annie.

Harriet heard Barbara Feigenbaum's chair scrape

the floor as she pushed it back, rising to go. Rats, she thought, scampering toward the staircase as quietly as she could manage. They were so *close*.

• • •

Harriet tried to sink back into her everyday spy routine, but it wasn't the same without Douglas and Balsam Fir. Or without Annie. I don't want to spend this much time by myself, she realized.

She called up Sport, who was happy to hear from her. "Been a long time," he said. "How was your New Year? Did you stay up till midnight and watch the ball drop?"

"Yeah. It was boring."

"It always is. I don't get New Year's Eve. It just seems like an excuse to get drunk and act stupid in public, for people who don't really *need* an excuse."

Harriet laughed. I've missed him, she thought. We agree about so many things. "You know what I did on New Year's Eve?" she said. "I read through a whole year's worth of spy notebooks."

"Really?" Sport sounded impressed. "How long did that take?"

"I don't really know. I fell asleep in my bed with the light on."

This time it was Sport's turn to laugh. "My dad does that every night. I used to go into his bedroom as soon as I woke up and turn it off for him. Sometimes I'd find him asleep in his chair with his face on the desk."

"Does Kate do that for him now?" Harriet lounged on her bed with the long cord stretched over her body, twisting it with her toe.

"I guess so." Sport sounded a little bit wistful. "The door's always closed. All I really know is what time he stops typing."

Harriet thought of the dinners she'd had at Sport's, how much she admired the quick bursts of rhythm when Matthew Rocque got up a real head of steam. She preferred peacock blue ink, but there was something very impressive about the mechanical tap dance of fingers that yielded a manuscript. "What are you doing tonight?" she asked Sport. "Would you want to come over or something?"

"Too much homework," he said. "And I'm baking a sourdough. I still have to knead it and punch it down after it rises. How about tomorrow, right after school? We could go to the park if it's nice out."

"I'd love it," said Harriet. "Have a good sourdough."

• • •

• • •

The next day was cold but not windy, so Sport and Harriet headed for Carl Schurz Park. A tugboat plowed through the East River, dragging a giant barge. The path along the embankment was still sunny next to the rail, though the pensioners sitting on benches looked frozen in place. Harriet felt strangely awkward with Sport as they strolled along the river. She wondered why, when she'd felt so completely at home with him on the phone. I'm not used to him being this *tall*, she decided. Sport had no right to grow so much faster than she did. It made her feel puny.

"Look at that gull," said Sport, pointing. A seagull was flapping right over the barge, so close that it looked like a kite tied to the stern with invisible string. "Why do you think he'd be flying like that?"

"Maybe he's riding a wind current."

"Maybe he's looking for dinner."

"Maybe he's a she." This is better, she thought, feeling loose again. That was the thing about really good friends: even when you'd been out of touch, you could pick up right where you left off.

"Maybe he isn't a seagull at all." Sport smirked. "He *might* be a very thin swan."

"Or an albino crow." The gull made a raucous,

rude squawk and flew away, as if it were offended. They both cracked up.

• • •

When the sun got too low and the park got too cold, they walked back toward Sport's, passing the playground where they had first met. A professional dog walker went by with an oddly assorted pack of lapdogs, retrievers, and an Afghan hound fanned out on leashes held in both hands.

"How do they *do* that?" asked Sport as they crossed the street in front of his building. "What if the dogs start to fight with each other?"

"They must hold auditions," said Harriet.

Sport grinned. "Imagine the rejects. 'I'm sorry, Mrs. Kessler, but your Lhasa apso does not play well with others. Little Wudgie has been expelled.' "

Harriet looked at him. "Sport? Why did Yolanda—Annie, I mean—get expelled from your school?"

"No idea. One day she was going to class and the next she was gone."

"It was Thanksgiving weekend, remember?"

"How could I forget?" said Sport gloomily. "It was the dawn of my heartbreak." He stuck his key in the door that led to his lobby and held the door open for Harriet. They started up the three flights of worn stairs to his walk-up apartment.

"How's Annie doing?" he asked, his voice tender.

"I wish I could tell you. She's not speaking to me."

"Why not?" They turned onto a landing.

"It's kind of a long story," Harriet hedged.

"Try me."

"I kind of spied on her. Followed her places when she didn't know it."

"Not cool," said Sport. "People's feelings get hurt."

"Tell me about it," said Harriet, trying to stifle the misery that had crept into her voice. They were outside the door to Sport's apartment, marked 4-C with brass figures. As he fiddled with upper and lower locks, Harriet gazed at the pattern the receding flights of stairs made below them. What's the right way to describe that? she wondered. Rectangular spiral? Maybe Matthew would have the right phrase.

Sport swung the door open. "I'm back," he called out. "With Harriet."

Kate emerged from the kitchen, wiping her hands on a towel she'd stuck in the waistband of her business suit as an apron. "Well, hello, stranger. We haven't seen you in way too long."

"Happy New Year," said Harriet awkwardly. Kate stood there smiling at her.

"Want to try some of my sourdough?" Sport said. "It came out pretty well."

"He's a genius," said Kate, clapping Sport on the back.

Sport shrugged. "Anybody can bake."

"That's what you think," said Kate. "Remember my buttermilk biscuits?"

"Those were kind of nasty." Sport grinned.

"Matthew loved them. Of course, he'd eat paperweights if he was writing. I'm going to go change my clothes before I spill tomato sauce all over myself. Make yourself at home, Harriet." She gave Harriet's arm a quick conspiratorial squeeze as she passed. What is *with* her? thought Harriet, flinching.

Sport went into the kitchen and sawed off two raggedy slices of bread. "Want it toasted?"

"Whatever you think."

"Plain with butter," he said, setting the bread on two plates and grabbing a butter knife. His back was to Harriet. "I'm sorry to hear about Annie. I know how you feel. I still miss Yolanda."

"That's different," Harriet said. "Yolanda's not real. Annie is."

"She was real to me," Sport said, unwrapping the butter.

"Sorry," Harriet muttered.

"It's okay," said Sport. "I'm sorry you're sad."

They looked at each other a moment. Then Sport

stepped forward and gave Harriet a stiff, clumsy hug. She backed away instantly, banging into the table so hard it hurt.

"What are you *doing*?" she practically screamed. "You're not supposed to do stuff like that! You're my *friend*!"

"I didn't mean—"

"This is just too . . . peculiar," said Harriet, still backing up.

"For God's sake," Sport snapped, "it was just a dumb hug. I've known you since we were both four!"

Harriet looked at him, cornered against the dishwasher. "We're not four anymore," she said. Her left side was throbbing where she had slammed into the table, and both of her ears felt unnaturally hot, as if they'd been toasted.

"Did you really think I was putting the moves on *you*? That's ridiculous!"

Harriet didn't answer. Sport was glaring at her, and she felt very small and embarrassed. She stared at her shoes and thought, I'll write about this someday.

"I'm in love with Yolanda, you jerk. You're my *friend*." Sport slammed Harriet's plate on the table in front of her. "Now eat this before I get mad."

Harriet did. It was excellent.

The very next morning, as she was brushing her teeth, Harriet made a decision. Annie had been freezing her out long enough. This whole thing was out of proportion—annoying, in fact. Harriet wasn't a double agent. She hadn't done anything wrong. I'm a spy, she thought defiantly; spying is what spies do.

She went back to her room, straightened her pale blue bedspread, got dressed in the clothes she'd already chosen, and looked at the clock. She still had ten minutes. She got out her latest green notebook and sat down to make a list of possible strategies.

PROBLEM: BEST FRIEND IGNORING ME

POTENTIAL SOLUTIONS:

1) LIVE WITH IT.

2) IGNORE HER BACK. LET HER SEE HOW IT FEELS.

3) YELL AT HER. WHO DOES SHE THINK SHE IS??

4) APOLOGIZE.

Harriet paused to reread her list. Option 1 was a bore. She'd already tried Living With It, and she'd had enough; that was why she'd made this list. She crossed it out.

Option 2, Ignore Her Back, had potential, but Annie was ignoring her so effectively that she might not even notice. Harriet crossed this out too.

Option 3, Yell At Her, had a lot of appeal. Harriet was extremely irritated that this had been going on so long, for more than a week now. She had plenty of steam to let off, and if she really let Annie have it, Annie would have to respond in some way. Probably by getting mad back, thought Harriet, deciding that 3 wasn't such a good option after all.

That left only option 4, Apologize, which presented its own set of problems. Harriet wasn't about to apologize for behavior she didn't regret. I *am* sorry that Annie's not speaking to me, she thought, but I'll never be sorry that I'm a spy.

"*Harriet!*" her mother called up the stairs. "You'll be late!"

Harriet closed her notebook, then opened it to write one final sentence:

PROBLEM NOT SOLVED.

• • •

Mr. Bolbach leaned on the blackboard, droning about polyhedrons. When he turned to draw an example, the back of his gray jacket was yellow with chalk dust, making him look like a human eraser. Harriet stifled a giggle, turning to see whether Annie had noticed. Annie gave her a look that would wither ripe fruit.

I'm sick of this, Harriet thought, reconsidering the Yell At Her option. She thought about throwing a spitball at Annie, the satisfying *thwack* it would make when it hit her between the eyes, right when she least expected it. *That* would show her that Harriet M. Welsch was not somebody you could ignore.

Harriet tore a page out of her assignment pad, moving in superslow motion so she wouldn't make noise, but before she was finished, the bell rang and Annie swept into the hall with the rest of the girls.

The next class was gym. Harriet hated gym at the best of times, but this was the worst: it was time for the annual Presidential Physical Fitness evaluations.

Harriet had already humiliated herself with her inability to climb a rope, do more than one pull-up, or swing herself into a long standing broad jump. Today she would get to be slower than anyone else at the shuttle run.

Why don't they rate us on things that kids actually *do*, thought Harriet, angrily pulling on sweat socks. I'd be in the ninety-ninth percentile at sledding or bike riding.

Annie was changing her clothes in the corner, with her back turned to Harriet. Marion and Carrie, who both took gymnastics and ballet after school, were yammering on about their gymnastics meets and the trophies they'd won. Harriet grimaced and tried to pretend they were inside an active volcano. Suddenly Marion's voice changed. "What's *that*?" she demanded in mocking tones.

Harriet turned. On the floor underneath the bench was an object she recognized instantly: Annie's sock monkey. Annie's backpack had tipped over onto the floor and the toy must have fallen out. Marion snatched it, grinning, bobbing it up and down.

"What wittle baby bwought *this* to school?"

Harriet caught a quick glimpse of the mortified, angry expression on Annie's face and said quickly, "That's mine."

Marion turned. Her smile was enormous, as if she

couldn't believe her good luck. "It's yours? Wittle Welsch dwopped her toy?"

"It's a treasured antique, if you don't mind." Harriet kept her voice even and held out her hand for the monkey. Marion cracked up.

"A treasured *antique*! Oh, in that case." She handed the monkey to Harriet. "You're going to need this when you suck your thumb."

Carrie cracked up and high-fived Marion. They went out of the locker room in fits of giggles. Annie and Harriet looked at each other. "Here," said Harriet brusquely, tossing the sock monkey to Annie and leaving the room.

Annie caught up with her on the starting line for the hundred-yard dash. Just before Coach Wiejazcka blew the whistle, she grabbed Harriet's hand for a split second, whispering, "Thanks, H'spy." The whistle shrilled, and they both charged for the finish line.

• • •

"How are the Birdlip Twins?" asked Annie as they walked away from the Gregory School.

"Dull," replied Harriet, glad that Annie was speaking to her again.

"Well of course they're dull. They wouldn't be Birdlips if they weren't dull. How about Fabio and Naima?"

"She dropped him."

"What?" Annie stopped in her tracks so abruptly that the second graders walking behind them nearly slammed into her. "What happened?"

"Fabio must have been cheating on her. I went up the fire escape to that window in back of the cleaners—the one that looks down on the tailoring section. Naima was cutting his jacket to pieces with pinking shears."

Annie's eyes were enormous. "His *motorcycle* jacket?"

Harriet nodded. "He dropped it off for a stain removal two days ago. I want to see his face when he comes back to pick it up."

"Let's go!"

"Sure," said Harriet, smiling with deep satisfaction. Annie doesn't mind spying when it's not on *her*, she was thinking. "Let's pick up a snack at the Koreans'. I still have some milk money."

• • •

They riffled through bags of chips. Annie favored the oddly shaped, glazed Japanese snacks with small flecks of seaweed, but Harriet insisted she try *plantanitos*. "They're made from fried plantains," she said. "They're like a cross between bananas and potato chips, only better."

"Fine," Annie said, "but I get to pick out the drinks." She went to the cooler and came back with two cans of papaya punch. Harriet narrowed her eyes. Had Annie developed a taste for papaya while meeting with P.'s kind-of-cute surfer bodyguard? She thought of him flashing that peace sign and saying, "Nice gloves," and felt instantly dizzy, as if she'd been spinning in circles too long. I've got to find out who he is, she thought, but this was hardly the moment to ask. Annie had just started speaking to her; the last thing Harriet wanted to do was get her angry all over again.

She took the two cans of papaya punch and the bag of plantain chips to the front counter, where Myong-Hee was leafing through a copy of *Vogue*. Over the register, next to the dollar bill that had been taped up there ever since Happy Fruit Farm had opened, Harriet spotted a Christmas card with a photo of dozens of baby pines planted in rows, and the message *Season's Greetings from Whitaker Christmas Tree Farms*. Underneath, someone had written with a red felt-tip pen, *Happy New Year to Myong-Hee, from Zane Whitaker (and Sam)*.

Harriet stepped on Annie's foot. "Ow!" Annie yelped, turning indignantly. Harriet tilted her chin with a look of significance. She had to do this twice more before Annie got it and peered at the card. She read it through, took a step back, and said, "Sam?" Harriet stepped on her foot again.

"*Stop* that!" said Annie. Harriet paid Myong-Hee as fast as she could and trundled Annie out to the curb before she could say anything incriminating.

"You need some poker-face lessons," she said.

Annie looked at Harriet, her face a mask of intense disappointment. "Douglas Fir's name is *Sam*. What a dull, normal name. There's no poetry in it. I *can't* be in love with a Sam."

"What happened to a rose by any other name smelling as sweet?"

"I can't make the leap." Annie shook her head.

"Are you someone different when you're Rosarita?"

"I *think* I am," Annie said. "Sometimes that's all you can have." She reached for the bag of plantain chips and set off down the sidewalk, angling her feet so she'd leave unusual footprints.

Harriet hurried to catch up and walked by her side, angling her feet in just the same way. "Twin clubfeet," she said.

"Ballet victims," Annie replied. "Third position for *life*." They limped side by side to the corner of East Eighty-seventh Street. Suddenly someone stepped out from between two parked cars.

Harriet's heart leaped. It was the surfer guy, and he

was wearing his fingerless gloves. He laid a hand on Annie's arm.

"Come with me," he said, in a low, urgent whisper. "Right now, before anyone sees you."

Annie turned wide eyes to Harriet. "Don't tell," she begged.

CHAPTER 12

Harriet didn't know what to do. It didn't *seem* like a kidnapping—Annie had gone of her own free will, and Harriet knew she had met the same man at least twice before—but something about the way he'd approached her felt wrong. She kicked herself mentally for not asking Annie more questions about the two men she'd been meeting. The cute guy always brings her to meet P., she thought. If I just had a clue who P. *was*.

She decided to stake out the Feigenbaums' house. Annie's rendezvous usually didn't last more than a couple of hours, since she didn't want to be caught by her uncle and aunt. So the Feigenbaums must not be in on the secret, Harriet realized as she thought back—Annie had set up both meetings with P. while they were away from their house. But now they were home, seeing patients. And this *wasn't* a meeting that Annie had planned—she had looked just as surprised as Harriet when the blond guy approached her. This made Harriet even more anxious. Annie might be in danger, she thought. I have to tell someone.

She went upstairs, hauled the phone into her bedroom, and closed her door. Luckily Sport was at home.

"Hi, Spy. What's up?"

Harriet didn't waste words. "Remember when your mother kidnapped you?"

"That isn't exactly the sort of thing you can forget," said Sport, whose horrid mother had once kept him prisoner in, of all places, the Plaza Hotel.

"I think maybe Annie's been kidnapped."

"Yolanda?" Sport yelped. Harriet gave him a rundown of what she had witnessed, and Sport agreed that it sounded awfully fishy.

"Let's meet at the Feigenbaums'," Harriet said.

• • •

Barbara and Morris sat them down on the couch of the waiting room. Their last patients were gone, and the doors to both offices stood open. Harriet could see Morris's couch in one room, across from a huge leather chair and a low table with one box of Kleenex. Across the hall, she caught a glimpse of Barbara's examining table, with a long roll of sanitized paper and stirrups. It gave her the shivers.

"What did he look like?" Barbara demanded.

"He's probably in his twenties. Shaggy blond hair with a little goatee. He wears fingerless gloves," she added significantly. Sport looked at her and she felt herself blush. "And one of those woven jackets from Central America. He's probably—how tall are you, Sport?"

"Five foot six," said Sport.

"He's maybe an inch or two taller. And he has a dimple right here," she said, placing her finger on one pink cheek.

Barbara and Morris looked at each other, bewildered.

"And you've seen him with Annie before?" Morris asked.

Harriet nodded. "Twice. She met him both times at the Papaya King, and he took her to meet with the other man, P."

"*Other* man?" Barbara demanded. "What other man? What do you mean by 'P.'?"

Morris set a calming hand on her arm. "Describe him, please, Harriet."

"Older," said Harriet. "Sandy brown curls and a long nose, like—"

Barbara jumped off the couch. "I knew it!" she shouted. "I *knew* he was going to sneak down here and see her. Oh, his goose is cooked. He'll be lucky if he gets a weekend. I'm going to call Jackie this minute!"

"Not till we find out—" Morris bellowed, but Barbara was already out of the room. "Who *is* he?" said Harriet. This was all going too fast.

Morris sighed. "Annie's father."

• • •

The police had been called, as had Harriet's parents. Morris Feigenbaum told the Welsches that Harriet was an important witness and would have to stay with them until the detectives arrived. *Detectives*, thought Harriet, frightened and secretly thrilled. She would get to be interrogated by a team of professionals. She wondered if there would be one who was hard-edged and mean and one who was pudgy and kinder, with a reassuring soft baritone, as there always seemed to be on TV shows.

Barbara came back in, babbling so quickly that

Morris went into his office and got her a tranquilizer. It seemed to have no effect. Harriet and Sport kept their seats on the couch, watching her pace on the waiting room carpet, nervously touching her earrings and ranting about Annie's father. "I told Jackie the first time she went on a date with him," Barbara said. "Once a shark, always. I knew he would leave her in tatters."

"You'll make yourself crazy," said Morris.

"If he harms one hair on her *head* . . . ," Barbara threatened.

"He's not going to harm her. He just wants to see his daughter."

"And my sister doesn't?" raged Barbara. "I'll tell you who I'd like to sue, is that judge who came up with this nonsense. The nerve of him, yanking that poor child away from both parents until they determine her custody. Heartless!" She was still bouncing back and forth, from one side of the room to the other. It was like watching a tennis match, Harriet thought, but with much better dialogue.

"We've been through this a million times," Morris was saying. "Jackie and Chris are behaving like wolverines."

Chris? Harriet wondered. Why would someone named Chris be called P.? But there was no more time to wonder since Morris was still talking. "It's better for Annie that she's been away from all that."

The front door had opened. "Away from all *what?*" said a voice from the hallway. "What's better for me?"

"*Annie!*" Barbara screamed. "Thank heavens you're safe." She launched her lean body at Annie as she appeared in the arch of the waiting room. Annie sidestepped her aunt, accusatory eyes landing on Harriet.

"You *promised* you wouldn't tell."

"I was worried," said Harriet. "I thought you'd been kidnapped."

"Wrong," Annie said, her voice icy.

"You've got some explaining to do, young lady," said Morris. "We've called the police."

"The *police?*"

"We didn't know where you were! How *dare* you make plans with your father! You know what the judge said!" shrieked Barbara. Morris tried to restrain her.

"Don't you dare try to shut me up!" she screamed, whirling on Annie. "What were you *doing* with him??"

"Eating Chinese food," said Annie. "Papa bought me an egg roll. Is that such a crime?" *Papa,* thought Harriet. P.

"The only good thing about this," Barbara said,

her eyes flashing, "is that that man will *never* get custody now."

Annie glared at her aunt. "That's what he drove here to tell me. The judge has decided that it's up to me."

Barbara staggered as if she might faint. "What?" she gasped. "How can he do that?"

"The law," Annie said, "is the law."

"Does your mother know about this?" Morris asked.

Barbara pushed him impatiently, stepping toward Annie. "Who are you going to go with?" she asked in a tremulous voice.

Everyone's eyes were on Annie. She surveyed the room slowly, then reached down to unzip her backpack with slow and deliberate drama. "I haven't decided as yet," she pronounced. "I need to consult with some people I know: Cassandra D'Amore, Yolanda Montezuma, and Rosarita Sauvage."

She took out her sock monkey and swept from the room with elaborate dignity, just as a voice called from outside, "*Police!*"

• • •

It was late by the time Sport and Harriet were finally sent home. "I wonder which parent Annie will pick?" said Sport.

"If her mother is anything like Barbara Feigenbaum, I'd go for P. He looked all right," said Harriet. She was dying to get home and write about the detectives; Captain Siri and Officer Wolford had not been at all what she'd pictured.

"Who would *you* pick?" asked Sport, stopping on the sidewalk in front of Harriet's house. "I mean, it's no contest for me—my mother is nuts, and I'd go with my father and Kate in a heartbeat—but who would you live with if you had to choose?"

Harriet searched her mind for an answer. Her father was more easygoing, and certainly funnier, but he was always at work. And she couldn't imagine not coming home to her mother's warm smile. What would it be like to live with just one of her parents? "I don't know," she said finally. "I'm glad I don't have to decide."

"Anyway, it doesn't matter," said Sport, sounding gloomy. "Annie's mother and father both live in Boston."

"That's true," Harriet said. "I didn't think of that. As soon as she makes up her mind, she'll be moving away."

They looked at each other a moment. Sport looks just as sad as I feel, thought Harriet, and without even thinking about it, she reached for his hand. "But we'll still have each other. As *friends*," she hastened to add, letting go of his hand.

"Of course as friends," Sport said. "What else would we be?"

• • •

The following weekend, Harriet went to the Feigenbaums' to help Annie pack her belongings into the trunk of their Volvo for the long drive back to Boston. Before Harriet left her room, though, she took out her notebook. Through assiduous spying on her mother and Barbara Feigenbaum, who had somehow become thick as thieves, Harriet had learned several important things, all of which she wanted to get down on paper.

FIRST OF ALL, ANNIE WAS LYING. SHE DOES NOT HAVE TO CHOOSE BETWEEN HER TWO PARENTS. THE JUDGE HAS ALREADY DECIDED THAT THEY'LL HAVE JOINT CUSTODY. SHE WILL LIVE WITH HER MOTHER ON WEEKDAYS AND P. (WHOSE NAME IS CHRISTOPHER SMITH) ON ALTERNATE WEEKENDS AND SUMMER VACATIONS.

ANNIE ALREADY KNEW ALL THIS WHEN SHE GOT BACK TO THE FEIGENBAUMS'. THAT'S WHAT HER FATHER WAS TELLING HER OVER THE EGG ROLLS AT MING MOON. SHE WAS

JUST TRYING TO GIVE HER AUNT BARBARA A HEART ATTACK (WHICH WOULDN'T BE HARD, FROM THE LOOK OF HER).

Harriet paused for a moment, then wrote, I BET ANNIE'S RELIEVED NOT TO HAVE TO DECIDE. I'D BE RELIEVED. She chewed on her pen and started another new paragraph.

SECOND, ANNIE WAS NEVER EXPELLED FROM SPORT'S PUBLIC SCHOOL. SHE HAD BEEN ON A WAITING LIST FOR THE GREGORY SCHOOL ALL ALONG, AND A PLACE OPENED UP AT THANKSGIVING WHEN IRIS MUTH MOVED TO SWITZERLAND.

THIRD, THE GUY IN THE FINGERLESS GLOVES IS THE SON OF CHRISTOPHER SMITH'S BUSINESS PARTNER. HIS NAME IS ELIAS AND HE GOES TO NYU FILM SCHOOL.

She could feel her ears starting to burn, so she picked up the pen and wrote quickly:

HE IS 23, WHICH IS ACTUALLY VERGING ON OLD. AND ACCORDING TO ANNIE, HE SAYS "UM" AND "LIKE" ALL THE TIME, WHICH IS SURELY A SIGN OF A LAZY MIND. EVEN IF HE HAS GREAT TASTE IN GLOVES.

FOURTH, I'M CONVINCED THAT ANNIE'S PARENTS LOVE HER. P. LOVES HIS DAUGHTER SO MUCH THAT HE BROKE THE

RULES SO HE COULD SEE HER, AND HER MOTHER LOVES HER SO MUCH THAT SHE FOLLOWED THE RULES, EVEN THOUGH SHE MISSED ANNIE LIKE CRAZY. OLE GOLLY TOLD ME THERE ARE ALL KINDS OF LOVE IN THE WORLD, BUT I THINK THERE'S JUST ONE, USING DIFFERENT IDENTITIES. JUST LIKE MY FRIEND ANNIE SMITH.

Harriet reread her list from the beginning, then paused for a moment to ask herself if there was anything else of importance to say. There was.

FIFTH, ANNIE LOVES TO WRITE LETTERS. THIS IS AN EXCELLENT THING TO FIND OUT WHEN SOMEBODY IS MOVING, ESPECIALLY WHEN YOU'RE A WRITER YOURSELF.

About the Author

Maya Gold, like Annie Smith, is a woman of many identities. In some of her other lives, she has been an award-winning screenwriter, novelist, editor, and occasional planter of Douglas firs. But her favorite role is that of proud mother to ten-year-old author and deep-dyed Harriet fan Sophia M. Gold. They live in New York.

About the Author of *Harriet the Spy*

Louise Fitzhugh was born in Memphis, Tennessee. She attended Bard College, studied art in Italy and France, and continued her studies in New York at the Art Students League and at Cooper Union. Her groundbreaking first children's novel, *Harriet the Spy*, was followed by *The Long Secret* and *Sport*, and all are acclaimed as milestones of children's literature. These classics delight children year after year.

About the Author

Maya Gold, like Annie Smith, is a woman of many identities. In some of her other lives, she has been an award-winning screenwriter, novelist, editor, and occasional planter of Douglas firs. But her favorite role is that of proud mother to ten-year-old author and deep-dyed Harriet fan Sophia M. Gold. They live in New York.

About the Author of *Harriet the Spy*

Louise Fitzhugh was born in Memphis, Tennessee. She attended Bard College, studied art in Italy and France, and continued her studies in New York at the Art Students League and at Cooper Union. Her groundbreaking first children's novel, *Harriet the Spy*, was followed by *The Long Secret* and *Sport*, and all are acclaimed as milestones of children's literature. These classics delight children year after year.